PUPPY LOVE AND PANIC

A TALKING DOG COZY MYSTERY

HEYWOOD HOUNDS COZY MYSTERIES
BOOK FOUR

CARLY WINTER

Edited by
DIVAS AT WORK EDITING
Cover By
COVEREDBYMELINDA.COM

WESTWARD PUBLISHING / CARLY FALL, LLC

In Dog Treats and Death:

When Gina Dunner's brother, Vic, is accused of murdering his ex-girlfriend, Gina isn't surprised. Living the life of a womanizing ranch hand with questionable friends and a lifetime of bad choices had to catch up with him at some point.

After the Sheriff announces she has the right man, Vic vehemently denies the murder. When he begs Gina to help prove his innocence, she attempts to puts her doubts aside, despite him being the last one to see the woman alive. She and her rescue mutt, Daisy—a sweet, yet sassy, talking dog—start sniffing around into their own investigation.

In Paw Prints and Problems:

When restaurant owner, Sally Turner, finds her chef murdered, she realizes she's in deep trouble... especially when she was the last one to see the victim alive and they'd been arguing when she left him. She turns to Gina for help in finding the real killer.

As Gina assists Deputy Trevor Hutchison exploration into the chef's past, they find a cast of unsavory characters, lies and danger. Amidst the investigation, an unexpected guest - a rambunctious golden retriever named Zeus - lands on Gina's doorstep. Juggling the search for a murderer and managing the mischievous canine tests Gina's patience, leading to conflict with those around her.

With her talking dog, Daisy, at her side, will Gina be able to find the destructive Zeus a suitable home and navigate the investigation without becoming a victim herself?

Meanwhile in Furballs and Fatalities...

When the owner of Hammer and Nail Hardware is found dead, Gina's most loyal customer, Erika, becomes the prime suspect.

Despite having every reason to kill Molly Burton, Erika vehemently denies involvement and pleads with Gina to help uncover the real murderer. With almost all evidence pointing to Erika, Gina and her talking dog, Daisy, along with Deputy Trevor Hutchinson, delve into the secrets concealed behind the aisles of the hardware store. However, the clues they unearth leave them with more questions than answers.

Adding to the chaos, Gina takes in a bonded pair of dogs who prefer solitude. Daisy is determined to break them up, despite Gina's pleas to let them be.

As danger escalates, can Gina and Daisy hammer out the details and expose the true murderer?

And now on to Puppy Love and Panic...

ABOUT THIS BOOK...

An innocent has never looked so guilty...

When a girl is found dead at an all-night house party, the sheriff accuses Gina's son, Jacob, of being the murderer.

Despite the evidence stacked up against him, Gina is determined to find the real killer and bring them to justice. However, her quest for the truth is complicated by two unexpected obstacles: the fluffy, blonde puppy unexpectedly in her care, and the return of her long-estranged mother.

As she works to track down the murderer with her talking dog, Daisy, at her side, Gina realizes that her unscrupulous family history just might come in handy in helping her solve the case.

But how far will a mother go to prove her child's innocence?

CHAPTER 1

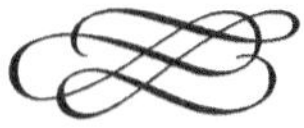

"You're really going out wearing that?" I asked, trying hard to hide my smile.

"It's a disco party, so yes," my son, Jacob said. "Annabelle told me this was a perfect outfit."

As I stared at him in his white flared pants, matching jacket and black button-down shirt open to his navel, it made sense that he'd go to the most eclectic person I knew to get the look right.

"Well, she was right." I sighed and crossed my arms over my chest. "What time will you be home?"

He'd arrived back from college for Spring Break two days ago, and it had been a whirlwind of activities for him while catching up with old friends and hanging out with those in the area who hadn't gone to California or Mexico. "I'm not sure, so don't wait up."

I gave him a quick once over as he pushed his blond hair out of his face. "You're missing one thing," I said. "I'll be right back."

I rarely wore jewelry, but somewhere along the way I'd picked up a thick, gold chain. After pulling it from a drawer, I hurried back to the living room to find Daisy staring at him.

"He looks kind of stupid," she said. "And I'm super sad he's going out again. I wish he'd stay home and snuggle with me. I think that would be way more fun for both of us."

I nodded, completely agreeing with my talking dog. I'd never say it out loud because I wouldn't want to guilt trip my kid, but I also wished he'd stay home. But, at nineteen, he was free to do what he wanted. On the other hand, Daisy would be perfectly fine laying on the guilt thicker than peanut butter. Good thing Jacob couldn't hear her.

"This will complete the look," I said. Standing behind him, I clasped the chain around his neck. "You may want to gel your hair back as well to complete the John Travolta look."

"The what look?"

"You have no idea who Annabelle has dressed you as?"

He shook his head and I pulled out my phone. On YouTube, I found a video of the iconic Saturday Night Live dance scene. When it ended, he laughed. "Yeah, I'm not dancing like that."

"I don't think you could if you tried," I muttered, watching the video again. "Very few men have moves like that."

Dang. Travolta knew how to gyrate those hips.

With a sigh, I clicked the phone off and smiled. "Are you going to do the hair?"

"I might as well," Jacob replied. "Can you help me?"

"Sure."

Daisy and I followed him down the hallway to the bathroom. Once there, I realized I wouldn't be able to reach the top of his head, so with the gel and comb in hand, I instructed him to sit on the edge of the tub while I stood inside it. Once I'd achieved the blond version of John Travolta, I said, "Take a look."

He stood and looked in the mirror, grimacing at his reflection.

"You look cute!" I said, stepping out of the tub.

"Whatever."

"Do you have any idea of what time you'll be home?" I asked, pressing the issue. I set down the gel and comb next to the sink.

"I don't know." He shrugged, and Daisy and I trailed behind him down the hall toward the front door. "It depends on who's there and if it's any fun."

"Okay, but don't do anything I wouldn't do."

He threw his head back and laughed. "That leaves pretty much everything wide open, Mom."

I rolled my eyes. Yes, I'd had a bit of a wild childhood, but most of the time, I found it to be an excellent idea to obey the law and stay out of prison. "Just don't do anything stupid."

"I won't," he muttered, then gave me a quick kiss on the cheek. "I'll see you when I see you. Love you."

"Bye, Jacob," Daisy called. "Miss you. I wish you'd stay home."

After tapping her on the head and taking my keys, my kid was off to live his best life.

"Is Trevor coming over?" Daisy asked as we walked back to the couch.

"Yes," I replied. "We're supposed to watch a movie."

I sat down, listening to the silence. Having my son home for Spring Break had been wonderful, and it made me realize how much I missed the constant chatter and his comings and goings. My only company while he was away at college was my talking dog, and sometimes I still wondered if me hearing her was a figment of my imagination.

Declaring my dog my only company was wrong. I'd been spending an awful lot of time with Deputy Trevor Hutchinson as well, to the point we'd fallen into some sort of dating pattern that I thoroughly enjoyed. It had taken me some time to realize our relationship had moved beyond friendship. That first kiss had knocked me silly. I didn't like to think about it all too much, but instead, I just enjoyed my time with him.

After flipping on the television, I hurried through the channels. So many of them that I didn't watch. Why in the world did I pay for cable these days when I had so many subscription services? Granted, Jacob had signed up for most of them when he lived at home. One of these days I'd have to go through my bills and figure out just how much I spent with the cable company and what I paid the subscription services. There were some I'm sure I didn't even realize I had.

Daisy snored softly beside me as I stroked her head and I watched a rerun of *Friends*. Tears of nostalgia welled in my eyes, especially when the death of Matthew Perry came to mind. Such a loss. Such a tragedy.

A little uncomfortable niggling weighed on me, but I couldn't place why.

Daisy sat up, her ears perked. She glanced around the room, then up at me. "Gina? I have a really bad feeling in my tummy."

Was I having conversations with myself? "It's okay," I murmured. "Everything's fine."

"Are you sure?" she asked. "Because I feel a little sick."

Frankly, so did I. It was in times like these that I questioned my sanity because my thoughts mirrored her words. "It must have been the egg salad."

"You wouldn't give me any egg salad. Remember?"

"But I saw Jacob slip you a little under the table," I said, scratching under her chin.

"You saw that?"

"I see everything, Daisy. I'm a mom. It's a superpower."

"My super sniffer is my superpower."

"Exactly. Just let me know if you need to go out." I turned my attention back to the television.

An hour passed while I chuckled along with the crew of *Friends*. I'd become so engrossed, I about jumped out of my skin when my phone rang.

"Who is it?" Daisy asked, her ears perking up once again.

"It's Trevor."

"Isn't he supposed to be here?" she asked.

"Yes. He's probably running behind because of work." I picked up the phone from the coffee table. "Hey, Trevor."

"I'm going to be late," he grumbled. "Sheriff Mallory called a meeting just as I walked in from a car accident on the highway."

"Was anyone hurt?"

"One guy needed to go to the hospital, but I think everyone is going to be fine." In the background, I heard Mallory. Just the sound of her voice made my skin crawl. "I need to go. She's screeching about something."

"You need to run against her," I said. "You'd make a great sheriff."

"And if I lose, I'm out of a job. She'd never allow me to keep working here."

"With me as your campaign manager, there isn't a chance of you losing."

"Gotta go. Don't know when I'll be there. Probably best to not count on me."

He hung up and I set my phone down with a long sigh of disappointment. Just me and my talking dog for now. It wasn't that I disliked hanging out with Daisy, but over the past few months, I'd really grown fond of Trevor and I had been looking forward to our evening.

We made a great team. Besides solving murders together, we enjoyed each other's company. He also made me laugh and Jacob seemed to like him as well. Would this cautious relationship ever lead to anything serious? I doubted it, but I was appreciating it while it lasted.

I sat through another hour of Friends and then clicked off the television. At eleven o'clock, I wasn't quite tired enough for bed, but I also didn't know what to do with myself.

I went into the kitchen and found my task. Me loving to have my child home for the week didn't mean I couldn't be irritated beyond belief that he used forty-five dishes a day, and left every single one of them in the sink instead of placing them in the dishwasher.

After I finished the dishes and wiped down the counters, my phone rang again.

"I'm not going to be there tonight," Trevor grumbled. "There's another accident. I'll try to swing by tomorrow."

Before I could speak, he'd disconnected.

I stared at my phone for a long moment. The weight of loneliness settled around me, causing my stomach to flip and my chest to feel heavy. "Maybe I should just go to bed," I announced to the empty house. Instead of dealing with my emotions, it seemed easier to sleep them away.

"Okay," Daisy said. "I'll beat you there!"

She took off down the hallway and I followed. Sleep finally came about an hour later, but my uneasiness never faded.

I DIDN'T KNOW what time it was when I heard someone pounding on my front door, but I was determined to ignore them. Until Daisy began to bark.

"Get up, Gina!" she yelled as she carried on. "There's a serial killer at the door!"

"Really?" I grumbled, throwing back the

covers. "I don't think serial killers announce their presence."

"That's probably true. But what if it's Jacob?" she said, jumping from the bed. "Maybe he forgot his keys!"

In my sleepiness, I'd forgotten he was home for Spring Break. I sprang up, grabbed my glasses and hurried to the front door. After checking the porch through the window, I saw that it was Trevor.

That uneasy feeling I'd had the previous evening became so heavy, my legs seemed to be made of cement as I opened the door.

"Trevor! Trevor!" Daisy yelled, dancing around his feet. "Trevor, pet me!"

"What happened?" I asked. As I studied his face, I noted the serious scowl. His hands clenched at his sides while his shoulders bunched under his uniform.

"I've been trying to call you," he said gruffly. "I need to come in."

"I didn't hear the phone." I stepped aside and when I shut the door, he took me into a long embrace. Tears welled in my eyes, even though I had no idea what he was about to say. Whatever it was, I understood it would alter my existence. I pulled away, hoping it had nothing to do with Jacob.

"What happened?" I asked again, crossing my arms over my chest.

"Let's sit down."

"No. Tell me right now."

He sighed and ran his thumb between his eyebrows. Finally, he met my gaze. "Gina, there's been a murder."

Oh, no. Where was Jacob? What time was it? I glanced out the window and noted the sun was on the horizon, almost ready to make its debut for the day.

He had left the previous evening for a night out with friends. He'd apparently been out all night, or...

I had to force myself to ask the question and I was terrified of what the response would be. "Is... is Jacob dead?" I always imagined I'd know if my son was no longer with me. I felt such an intricate connection to him, surely I'd instinctively be aware of his death.

"No! No," he said, placing his hands on my shoulders. "Jacob is... Jacob's down at the emergency clinic sleeping off one heck of a bender."

Relief flooded through me, but it only brought on more questions. Unless something had drastically changed, my son wasn't a big drinker. "What does that mean?"

"They couldn't wake him at the party, so they took him to the clinic."

Bile rose in my throat. "Is he okay?"

"They say he's going to be just fine, but he's in trouble."

I furrowed my brow. "Why is he in trouble?"

"Look, Gina. Here's the deal. Last night there was a big house party out at the Willard place. When the kids came to this morning, they found a young woman dead. She'd been strangled."

I nodded, the pain of a young life lost lancing through me. But that didn't explain why my son was in trouble. "What does that have to do with Jacob?"

"He... he was found passed out next to her with one end of the rope in his hand, the other wrapped around the girls' neck."

The room began to spin. I grabbed the wall to steady myself.

"Jacob wouldn't do anything like that," Daisy said. I glanced down to find her at my feet. "Jacob is a good dog, like me."

"What... what does that mean?" I asked, meeting Trevor's gaze.

He shrugged and ran a hand through his

blond hair. "It means that Sheriff Mallory thinks she's got the killer."

CHAPTER 2

RAGE EXPLODED within me with such force, I saw stars before my eyes while I continued to grip the wall. "Jacob had nothing to do with this," I hissed.

"I'm sure he didn't," Trevor said evenly. "But Mallory thinks he did and I wanted to be the one to tell you what was going on."

"Gina, you have to help Jacob," Daisy said.

"I want to see my son," I growled.

"You can see him when he wakes up."

"No. Now."

I marched down the hallway and quickly changed into a pair of jeans and a sweatshirt, then grabbed my sneakers and returned to Trevor.

"I want to see Jacob and then I'm going to

find out who's responsible for this tragedy, because it isn't my son. Aren't there cameras at the house? Everyone has their homes wired up to the hilt these days!"

"No cameras that we could find," Trevor said calmly. "It's probably best if you stay out of it."

"No! Mallory will happily railroad him and I'm not going to allow that to happen! Now, you either take me to the emergency clinic or I'm driving myself!"

My voice had taken on a high-pitched tone of complete panic and my hands began to shake. If I was going to help Jacob, I needed to rein in my anxiety. The tears I held back wouldn't do him any good. To save him, I needed to take action.

"Jacob took your car, Gina," Daisy said quietly. "You'll have to walk there."

Excellent point.

"Gina, you need to let me do my job," he said softly.

"Listen up, Trevor." I pointed a shaky finger at him. "You're either going to help me, or you're going to get out of my way. There is *nothing*, I repeat, *nothing*, that I won't do to clear my son. Do you understand me?"

"Gina, are you okay?" Daisy asked, then

she began to whine. "I've never seen you this upset."

"Here's the deal," Trevor said. "I think it's best that—"

"I don't care what you think," I hissed. "I'm going to the emergency care clinic right now."

"Trevor, I don't think you should argue with her," Daisy said. "She's so upset, she may kill you and stuff your body in a closet."

She wasn't wrong. I was very close to spinning out of control and felt such an urgency to get to my son, my insides vibrated. "Now, are you driving me, or are you getting out of my way?"

Trevor sighed heavily. "Okay, let's go."

"Bye, Gina," Daisy said. "I'll miss you and I promise to be a good dog."

I bent over and gave her a quick kiss on the nose, then Trevor and I hurried out the door. Part of me was relieved he'd acquiesced to my demands. I was so upset, I didn't think I could drive, even if I had a car.

Heywood didn't have a proper hospital. All the severe cases were taken to the hospital in Sedona. The fact that Jacob was at the emergency clinic let me know there was nothing seriously wrong with him. But dang it. What had he gotten himself into?

When we pulled up in front of the clinic, I jumped out of Trevor's truck before it came to a complete halt and ran inside. The smell of antiseptic assaulted me, but I grimaced and brushed it away.

"Where's Jacob Dunner?" I asked the receptionist, a young, blonde woman who had a love for houseplants. They sat on the counter around her, some of them so big, I wouldn't be able to see her if I moved to the right angle.

"You'll have to take a seat," she said, not looking up from her computer. She tapped a large stack of manila folders to her left. "We're very busy right now."

I turned to find six people in the waiting room, most of them staring at me. "I want to see my son."

"You'll have to wait."

"I have to wait to see *my son*, who is a patient here?"

She didn't bother answering. Instead, she pointed to the chairs. An argument hung on the tip of my tongue, but I held it. Every now and then I remembered speaking my mind wasn't the smartest thing to do.

With a curse, I pulled out my phone and

began to pace. I knew one of the nurses at the emergency clinic, so I texted her.

HI, Jillian. Jacob is here as a patient. This kid at the reception desk won't allow me to see him. Can you pull some strings?

AS I STARED at the screen and waited for a reply, Trevor came in.

"Thanks for waiting," he muttered.

"Sorry. I have to see Jacob. I have to make sure he's okay."

"They won't let you back?" he asked.

I shook my head and pointed to the receptionist. "She says I have to wait."

"We brought in four other kids in the same condition as Jacob," Trevor replied. "They may be a bit overwhelmed."

A moment later, the doors leading to the back swung open and Jillian appeared. In her late forties, I'd never seen her without her brown hair in the long ponytail down her back. Today she wore blue scrubs that strained over her hips. She met my gaze and waved me forward.

"We're really busy," she said as I brushed

past her with Trevor in tow. "These stupid kids and their drugs." She shook her head. "After they all come to, I'm going to beat them unconscious."

"They're on drugs?" I clarified.

"We don't know which ones, but all the evidence points to it. We're waiting for toxicology reports on all of them."

As we hurried down the short hallway, I glanced in the rooms. Most had families gathered around the bed, but I couldn't see the patients.

"Jacob's in here," she said, pointing to a room to the left.

I stared at the door for a long moment, suddenly deathly afraid of what I was going to find, despite Trevor's assurances Jacob was okay.

"He's resting right now, Gina," Jillian said, placing her hand on my shoulder. "I promise you, he's going to be fine."

With a nod, I pushed the door open. Swiping away tears, I hurried over to my son. Lying in the hospital bed with closed eyes, he looked dead. His cheeks were a little pale, but when I grabbed his hand, I found it warm.

"Jacob?" I whispered. "Jacob, honey? Can you hear me?"

I noted he was hooked up to an IV and I glanced over at Jillian, who stood in the doorway. "It's saline," she said. "Just to help get whatever he ingested flushed from his system."

Jacob groaned and I squeezed his hand. He clenched my fingers lightly in return. The tears fell as relief washed through me. He was going to be fine.

"Let me get you a chair," Trevor said softly.

I shook my head. "I'll just sit on the edge of the bed."

As I settled in, I studied Jacob's face. Now that I knew he was going to be okay, I considered the circumstances. Why in the world had he taken drugs? How long had he been doing so? Was it an everyday thing for him? Did he need rehab?

We'd always been close. I hoped that when he woke, he'd be honest with me and I'd do whatever I could to help him. Maybe I needed to put in a call to Annabelle. She'd helped her now boyfriend, Doug, get off drugs, and he'd literally been living under the local bridge shooting up on a daily basis.

"I'll be back soon," Jillian said. "If anyone gives you any flack about being back here, just tell them to come see me."

Turning to her, I nodded. "Thank you. I

really appreciate your help. I owe you big time."

She smiled and hurried away. I had no doubt she'd collect.

"Are you feeling a bit better?" Trevor asked.

"Yes." I sighed and shut my eyes. I didn't pray much, but I did send up a quick word of thanks. "I can't believe he took drugs. All those lectures that I gave, all those documentaries I made him watch... and he goes and overdoses."

Trevor placed his hand on my shoulder and gave it a squeeze. "I'm surprised as well. However, one thing I've learned through all these years of police work is that kids are different when their parents aren't around."

"He's never been in trouble, though." I shook my head. "Something doesn't seem right."

I squeezed Jacob's hand again as silence fell around the room. In the hall, people were hustling and bustling about. I had a hard time believing Jacob did drugs, but what was even more unbelievable was the notion that he killed that girl.

"Who died?" I asked.

"Ava Willard."

I furrowed my brow and glanced over my

shoulder at him. "Didn't you say the party was at the Willard place?"

"Yes."

"So she threw a party and someone killed her?"

"That's right."

"Where were her parents?" I asked.

"They weren't home. One of the kids I interviewed said they'd gone to Phoenix for the night and would be back some time today."

I lowered my head, the gravity of the situation causing my shoulders to slump. "Have you been in contact with them?"

"They're on their way back now." He pulled out his phone and glanced at the screen. "They're supposed to go directly to the sheriff's department so I can interview them. They should be arriving anytime."

"Who killed that poor girl?" I asked. "It wasn't Jacob. I don't even recall him mentioning her. I don't think he knew her."

"We'll ask him about it when he wakes," Trevor replied.

Voices in the hallway seemed to be coming closer. I expected their owners to walk by the room as they'd done previously. To my surprise, our door opened.

I turned to find Sheriff Mallory Richards,

and my spine stiffened. Slowly, I stood and walked around the bed, placing myself between her and my son. The hair on the back of my neck bristled as I clenched my fists at my sides.

"Ah, Gina," she said, smiling. The woman was my height, but muscular. In her fifties with short black hair, there probably wasn't a person on this earth that I detested more.

"Hello, Sheriff," Trevor said, standing next to me. "Gina was just checking in on her son."

"Oh, you mean my killer?" she asked. Glancing around me, she stared at Jacob a moment. "I shouldn't be surprised he's a drug abuser considering he's a Dunner."

Of course she'd bring up my family history. It wasn't too long ago that I discovered my father and brother had once been neck deep in the drug trade in Arizona. Thankfully, both were now out.

Instead of attempting to scratch her eyes out, I smiled. "What can I do for you?"

"I'm here to cuff him."

"Is that necessary?"

"Yes. Once he's awake, we'll take him to the station and book him for the murder of Ava Willard. Her parents will be pleased by how efficiently the Sheriff's Department has solved the murder of their little girl."

She attempted to step around me, but I moved to my left, blocking her. "My son had nothing to do with that horrible killing," I said between clenched teeth. "Do your job, and you'll find that out."

Mallory threw her head back and laughed. "He was found passed out next to the girl with a rope in his hand. Guess what, Gina? The girl was strangled with a rope." She shook her head as her smile faded. "I *have* done my job, and your son is going down."

CHAPTER 3

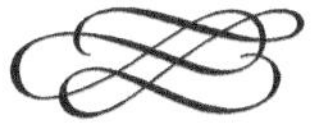

TREVOR HELD my elbow as she moved past me. I shook so badly, I was sure everyone in the room could hear my bones rattling. When the click of the cuffs sounded, I shut my eyes.

Don't kill her. Don't kill her.

"I've instructed the nurses to call me when he wakes," Mallory said, once again coming into my line of vision. "I'll be back for him then."

As she swooped out the door, I released a long, slow breath I hadn't realized I'd been holding.

"Gina, I need you to keep your head," Trevor said. "I thought you were going to attack her."

"I was."

"That's not going to do Jacob any good."

I yanked my arm out of his grasp. "And that's the only reason why I didn't rip out her heart and use it for soccer practice." Returning to the side of the bed, I took a couple of deep breaths. What should be my first step? My mind was such a jumbled mess. My motherly instincts told me to stay put with Jacob, but the urge to find the killer and get my son out of trouble overwhelmed me. I had to discover who killed Ava before Mallory began railroading Jacob.

To do that, I needed information. I stared at Jacob and willed him to wake up while also realizing that me staying with him accomplished my first steps. I was with him and once he came to, I'd have a chance to find out exactly what happened the prior night. I'd gather my information, which would send me on my hunt for the killer.

I concentrated on him so hard, I almost forgot Trevor was still in the room.

"Do you want some coffee?" he asked.

I nodded. "That would be great. Thanks."

He left silently, the sound of the door clicking the only indication that he was gone.

"Please wake up," I whispered, grabbing

Jacob's hand in mine again, still shocked at the thought that my son would take drugs.

Trevor returned a few moments later and Jacob groaned again just as I took my coffee cup. "Jacob?" I whispered.

His eyelids fluttered, and a moment later, his gaze met mine. "Mom?" He looked around, his brow furrowing. "What... where am I?"

"The emergency clinic," I said. My heart soared as the tears once again started to fall. Dang it. I hated crying.

He attempted to sit up, then winced. As he tried to bring his hand to his head, the handcuffs clinked against the metal bed railing. My rage returned as his eyes widened.

"What the heck?" he whispered.

"Jacob, I need to know what happened last night," I said, trying to keep my voice steady.

"Why am I in handcuffs?" he asked. "Why am I here? And why does my dang head hurt so bad?"

"Lay down," Trevor said. He came to my side and pushed a button on the bed. The back rose to support Jacobs' upper body. "Get comfortable, and let's talk, okay?"

Once the bed was in the proper position, Trevor moved his pillow upward and Jacob settled in against it. "What is going on?" he asked. "Someone please clue me in!"

Trevor pulled up a chair next to the bed and sat down. "Jacob, there was a murder at that party you went to last night."

His gaze darted from the handcuffs back to Trevor. "Who... who was killed?"

"Ava Willard," I said. I laid my hand on his calf and gave it a squeeze. "We need you to tell us everything that happened last night. We also need to discuss why you took drugs, but that can wait."

"Drugs?" he asked incredulously. "I didn't take drugs!" With his free hand, he rubbed his forehead. "I feel like I've woken up in another dimension."

"You've been passed out for hours," I said. "You definitely took drugs, Jacob. They're running toxicology reports to figure out which ones, so you can quit the innocent act."

"Can we get back to the murder?" Trevor asked.

Jacob stared at me for a long moment, then pursed his lips. When he spoke, his tone was low and more serious than I'd ever heard it. "I swear to you on my life that I didn't take any drugs."

His sincerity caught me off guard. Serenity

blanketed me when I realized he was absolutely telling the truth. I glanced over at Trevor, who didn't meet my gaze.

"You were pretty out of it, dude," he said. "Are you sure you didn't indulge a bit?"

"Trevor, I didn't." His head flopped back against the bed while he fisted the blanket with his free hand. "What can I say to make you guys believe me?"

"Why don't you start at the beginning, honey?" I said gently. "Tell us about the party and everything that happened."

"I need to read you your rights," Trevor said.

My hackles bristled once again. "Why?" I asked.

"Because I'm here not only as Jacob's friend, but as a cop." Trevor sighed, obviously irritated with the situation. "I'm gathering information on the investigation."

I shot to my feet. "No. Absolutely not. Get out, Trevor."

"Gina, I—"

"I told you before that you are either going to help me, or get out of my way. Jacob isn't saying a word to you."

"Mom, it's okay," Jacob said. "Really. I

don't have anything to hide. I didn't do anything."

My gut instinct screamed to kick Trevor out, but then again, if Jacob shared his story, perhaps it would clear him.

I slowly sat down on the bed again. "Are you sure?"

"I'm positive."

After Trevor read him his rights, Jacob took a deep breath and began his tale.

"We arrived at the party about nine," he said. "I went with Eric and Liam."

"How many people were there?" Trevor asked.

"At that time, about thirty."

"What was going on?" I asked.

Jacob shrugged. "There was disco music playing, some people were dancing, but most were out in back by the keg. The Willards have a big, grassy yard that slopes down into a creek. It's really pretty. Lots of big trees… it's nice."

"Did you know anyone there besides Eric and Liam?" I asked.

"Yeah, most of the kids were from around this area. A few were from the college, and some I didn't know."

"Did you know Ava well?" I asked.

He shook his head. "Not really. We've had a

class or two together, but I haven't spent a lot of time talking to her. She's a little out of my league."

"What does that mean?" I asked. "What league is she in that you aren't?"

"She was really pretty, super smart and popular, Mom." He shrugged. "Just not someone who would be interested in dating me."

"You *are* all those things," I said, pushing a strand of hair out of his face. It was still stiff from all the gel I'd combed through. "Would you have been interested in dating her?"

"Probably not." He sighed. "This is going to sound corny, but she... she was like the sun, Mom. People gravitated to her. She was the center of everything. I wouldn't want to be in her inner circle. It would be too... too much. I don't know how to explain it."

I nodded slowly, understanding perfectly. Jacob took after me. We preferred to be on the outskirts looking in, not front and center of the mix.

"What was the vibe of the party?" Trevor asked.

Jacob shrugged. "It was pretty chill until about midnight. A group of guys showed up and Ava's boyfriend got really upset. It looked like there was going to be a fistfight, but the group eventually left."

"What were they arguing about?" Trevor asked. He reached into his back pants pocket and pulled out a small notebook and pen.

"Something about Ava cheating on her boyfriend with one of them."

"What's Ava's boyfriend's name?" I asked.

"Oliver Ledger. He's some dude from just outside of town. He seemed nice, but he was really angry when those other guys showed up."

"Did you get the name of the guy she may have cheated with?" I asked. This could be a huge lead and clear Jacob!

"I think someone called him Gabe." He shut his eyes. "My head really hurts."

I squeezed Jacob's knee again, hoping to offer him support. "What was Ava doing while her boyfriend was fuming?"

"She was with her friends. Eric, Liam and I just sat back on the grass and watched the drama."

Trevor jotted down notes. "Did Gabe and Oliver fight?"

"Not that I saw. I mean, Ava's place is huge. There could've been something going on inside and I'd never know about it."

"It sounds like you, Eric and Liam kind of kept to yourselves," I said.

"We were talking to people, but we weren't part of any commotion."

"Was there more that happened?" Trevor asked.

"Ava was mad that a girl she didn't like showed up. She made a big deal about her being there."

"Who was that?"

"Her name was Zoe. I can't remember her last name. She and Ava were on the debate team together, and supposedly there was a lot of competition there. They didn't like each other at all."

"Make a note to find out Zoe's last name," I said, pointing at Trevor.

"Yes, ma'am," he mumbled while shaking his head.

"What else happened at the party?" I asked.

Jacob stared at the ceiling for a long while. "I don't know. Around two or three I started to get really tired."

"How many beers did you have?" Trevor asked.

"None."

Trevor and I exchanged glances. Was Jacob

worried he would be in trouble with me, or the deputy, if he answered truthfully?

"Honey, it's okay if you had a few beers," I replied. "You're old enough to go to war, so you're old enough to have a beer."

"The law says otherwise," Trevor interjected. "But, I happen to personally agree. You aren't going to get in trouble. I'm just trying to figure out your state of mind."

"None. I had zero beers. They had bottled water, so I stuck to that."

I furrowed my brow. "Are you sure?"

"Yes."

I stared at him for a long moment. "Jacob, when they found you, they couldn't rouse you, honey. You swear you didn't take drugs, and now you're saying you didn't drink. If all that's true, then why couldn't they wake you?"

Silence fell over the room, except for the constant commotion in the hall. Then it hit me.

If Jacob was telling the truth, that could only mean one thing: someone had drugged him.

"Think about when you started to feel tired," I urged. "Who was there? What happened?"

"Like I said, it was late. Almost everyone was gone. There were only a few of us there."

"What were you doing?"

"There was a fire pit out back, so we were sitting around it. Ava was there. It was her house. Eric stayed, but Liam had gone home. Oliver, Ava's boyfriend, was still around, but I think that guy Gabe and his friends had left. If they were still there, then they had to be inside."

"Do you remember who else was there?" Trevor asked, furiously scribbling in his notebook.

"Zoe was," Jacob mumbled as he furrowed his brow. "Eric has a crush on her, so that's why we didn't go home when Liam did."

"Think carefully about this, Jacob," I said. "What happened right before you started feeling tired?"

"I remember thinking I was ready to get home. The keg was gone, so everyone was drinking soda or water. This other girl... what was her name... maybe Terry? Anyway, she brought out water bottles and gave them to everyone sitting around. That's really the last thing I remember."

My heart pounded as the door opened and Jillian walked in. "I'm glad you're awake," she said, smiling. "I just need to get some vitals from you."

I could barely breathe while she wrapped the blood pressure cuff around his arm. This Terry person had drugged my son. At a minimum, she'd given him the water bottle that held the drugs. "Jillian, when are you getting the toxicology report back?"

She didn't answer until she was done with the blood pressure. "Looks good. We should have it back in another few hours."

I nodded, then motioned to her to follow me to the door. "I know you're supposed to call Mallory when Jacob wakes, but I was wondering if you could hold off for a while?"

She glanced over my shoulder at him.

"I'm not asking you to defy Mallory," I said. "I just need some time. She's got him cuffed to the bed, so he's not going anywhere."

After a long moment, she nodded. "Okay. I can wait an hour or two."

"Thanks a lot. I appreciate it."

As she opened the door and left, I pulled my phone out of my pocket and scrolled through my contacts. It was time for me to hire a lawyer.

CHAPTER 4

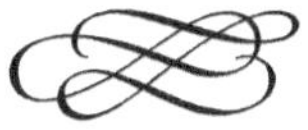

"Colin Breckshire III, at your service."

I smiled at the voice on the other end of the phone line. Elderly with a panache for wool suits, bowties and fedoras, he'd been a staple in the area for as long as I could remember. Although Colin wasn't a criminal attorney, he'd stepped in when I'd been accused of murdering my ex-husband and handled my case beautifully. I was hoping he'd do the same for Jacob.

"It's Gina Dunner," I said. "I need some help."

"Ah, Ms. Dunner. What a lovely surprise. Who are you accused of killing now?"

I laughed despite the seriousness of my situation. "No one. It's my son who's in trouble."

After explaining what Jacob had shared about the party and how he'd been found, Colin said, "And Mallory has him dead to rights, I take it?"

"She thinks she does."

He clicked his tongue. "I'm not a criminal lawyer, as you know, but I'll be happy to match you with a friend of mine, and until he can get into town, I'll represent your son."

With a sigh of relief, I nodded. "Yes. Thank you. The nurses here were supposed to call Sheriff Mallory when Jacob woke, but I've bought a couple of hours before they do."

"Excellent. I'll be right over to the emergency clinic. May justice prevail for the young Jacob Dunner!"

As I clicked off, I glanced around the room. The urge to make a list of things that needed to be done overwhelmed me. First, I wanted to talk to this Terry woman and find out why she'd drugged my son. Perhaps it had been a mistake and she handed him the wrong water bottle? If so, I'd throttle her for thinking it was a good idea to drug anyone.

"Listen, we also brought in one of Ava's friends, Bianca," Trevor said. "She's down the hallway. I figure if Jacob is awake, she may be, too. I was thinking I'd go talk to her."

I glanced at my son. Yes, I wanted to speak to Bianca, but I wouldn't leave Jacob unattended.

"I'll stay here," I said.

Trevor nodded and hurried from the room.

As I glanced around, I attempted to breathe through the panic that rose within me. I couldn't allow Jacob to go to jail. A bad idea began to form. What if I busted him out of the emergency clinic and hid him somewhere?

I carefully thought through the plan and raced over to the window. It opened enough for a person to get through it. If I called my brother, Vic, and had him bring over a saw to cut through the cuffs, then he could scuttle Jacob away through the window and hide him until all of this blew over.

Trevor would kill me for even thinking about it, and what about Mallory?

When she returned and her suspect was gone, she'd be looking for someone to skin. That would most likely be me.

Unless... unless I was somewhere else and I had an alibi at the time of Jacob's disappearance. When it all unraveled, I could be as confused and upset as everyone else. No one needed to know my plan.

"Mom?"

I turned to Jacob.

"I didn't have anything to do with Ava's death. I need to make sure you believe me."

"I do." I walked over to his bed and sat down. "I don't want you to go to jail. Having been there myself, it's not a great place to be. Mallory is coming for you." I pointed to the cuffs.

"I know."

"What do you think about getting out of here and going into hiding for a while?"

He pulled on his restrained wrist. "And how is that going to work?"

"I have an idea," I said. "Just give me the word, and I'll put the plan into action. We need to move quickly though." I glanced at my phone. "Jillian is going to call Mallory and tell her you're awake in about an hour and a half."

"Would I be breaking the law?" he asked.

"Oh, yes. Definitely. But while you're safe, I'd be working to get the evidence needed to clear you of this horrible crime."

Unlike me, Jacob was a rule follower. Although I had almost convinced myself that my bad idea would actually be beneficial to him, he had to go willingly. Of course, I could drug him again and have him taken to safety, but that plan may be headed straight into psycho-mom territory.

"So, if I get caught, I'd be in more trouble than I already am?"

"Yes. But you won't get caught. I promise."

He shut his eyes for a long moment, most likely weighing the pros and cons. Finally, he met my gaze. "Okay. I don't know how you're going to do this with me being cuffed to the bed, but let's go."

With a grin, I dialed Vic and once again paced the room.

"What's up, Gina?" he answered.

"I need your help."

As I explained Jacob's predicament again, Vic cursed and it sounded as if he was hitting something.

"That stupid son of a—"

"Call her names later," I interrupted. "Right now, I need you to come get Jacob out of here and put him somewhere the cops won't find him."

"I know just the place. We've got—"

"Don't tell me! The less I know, the better off I'm going to be during questioning. Jacob's room is on the south side of the emergency clinic. Once you're here, I'll open the window and then you two disappear."

"On my way, Gina. Don't you worry, though. I'll take good care of our youngest Dunner."

I had no doubt that he would. As I went over the plan with Jacob, I paced. My panic had been replaced by nervous butterflies.

"Do you think it'll work?" he asked, doubt lacing his voice.

"I do."

"Okay." He sighed deeply. "I'm just going to rest and try to get rid of this headache."

"That's a good idea."

He shut his eyes and shook his head. Tears slipped down the sides of his face. "I keep waiting to wake up from this mess, Mom. Like it's a bad dream or something. I didn't kill anyone, especially Ava. I didn't have any reason to."

I hurried back to his bedside and grabbed his hand. "I know, Jacob. You're nineteen, but let me step in and take care of this, okay?"

"Yep. Thanks, Mom. I'm scared to death."

I didn't have the heart to tell him that I felt the same.

~

VIC TEXTED me when he arrived. I stood, hurried to the window and slid it open. A moment later, he exited a pickup truck I didn't recognize parked in back and trotted over to me with a small saw in his right hand and clothing in his left. Had he stolen the vehicle? It was probably best I didn't know.

"Hey," he said as he easily hauled his bulky body through the window, then leaned over and kissed my cheek. He turned to my son. "Jacob! My man, you've got yourself in a bit of trouble, I see."

"Yeah."

"Keep your voice down, Vic," I said. I walked across the room and glanced out the door to the hallway. I didn't see any immediate threat to my plan, so I turned back to my brother. "Thanks for doing this."

"We're family, Gina. We take care of each other. Now go get an alibi. I've got this."

"What if someone comes in while you're sawing?"

"I guess I'll be sharing a cell with my nephew." He winked at Jacob, then picked up his restrained hand. "Piece of cake." As he fired up the small saw, I was surprised at how quiet it was. A second later, he'd cut through the chain, but the cuff remained on Jacob. "We'll get that off later. Now go, Gina."

Jacob stood from the bed and grabbed the clothes Vic had brought for him.

I really needed to leave. "Bye, honey. I'll see you soon."

"Love you, Mom."

As I slipped from the room, I knew I was doing the right thing, no matter how dangerous it may be. Getting Jacob out of the emergency clinic and away from Mallory until I could solve the murder was the best thing for him, and for me. If I knew he was safe, I would be able to concentrate.

I needed an alibi, but it couldn't be someone as obvious as my friend, Annabelle. Mallory would see right through that. Instead, I needed to be in a public place where numerous people would remember me, which also meant I had to cause a scene.

Cup of Go seemed perfect. I didn't have any friends there, but the baristas knew me since I was a semi-regular customer.

As I walked down the hall, I also realized I needed people to see me exit the emergency clinic. Jillian had been so nice in letting me back to see Jacob, and I didn't want to involve her any more than I already had. I decided to make sure the receptionist recalled me very well.

When I came to her desk, I stopped and smiled.

She glanced up at me. "Yes?"

"Do you have the time?"

"It's just after nine."

"Great. Thank you. And could you tell me what kind of plant this is over here?" I pointed at one, but didn't really see it. "It's very pretty."

"That's an ivy." She turned to the phone as it blared. Two lines lit up.

"One last thing," I said. "Has anyone else come by for my son, Jacob Dunner? I had hoped his grandfather or my friends would care enough to stop by."

"No. Not that I'm aware of. Now if you'll excuse me, I need to answer these calls."

"You really find out who cares in times like these," I said. She glared at me. "Sorry. Go ahead and get the phone."

As she answered, I hurried through the waiting room and exited the building. She'd announced the time, while I'd given Jacob's name and annoyed her. If she didn't remember me when she was questioned, she was just plain dumb.

The crisp, spring air actually felt nice

against my skin as I walked to Cup of Go, giving me clarity. Yes, I'd broken the law, but I knew in my heart that I had done the right thing. I'd walk through cut glass with my hair on fire to save my son from that stupid tyrant we called our sheriff.

Thankfully, the line inside Cup of Go wasn't too long. I waited patiently until it was my turn. "Good morning," I said to the young woman behind the counter.

"Hi. The usual?"

"No. Let's change it up today. How about a vanilla latte with some cinnamon?"

"That's new for you," she said while ringing me up.

"I'm trying to expand my taste in coffee, but I'm afraid that may be too sweet. What do you think? Should I change it to caramel?"

Her smile faded. "Well, caramel is sweet as well. Maybe you should stick to your Americano?"

"Maybe I should," I said. How could I be a bigger pain? "Or maybe I should try a cappuccino today!"

Her smiled faded again as the man behind me cleared his throat. "Maybe you should step aside until you have a better idea of what you would like," she suggested.

"No, I'm good. I'll have the vanilla latte." I turned and grinned to the man behind me. "Sorry. I'm a little indecisive today."

When the barista brought me the coffee, I dug through my purse looking for some cash, which I knew I didn't have. I figured it would be another detail for when she recalled our interaction later.

I apologized again, then handed her my credit card. Just before she ran it, I said, "Did I give you the right one? What's the name on it?"

The barista looked at the card. "Gina Dunner."

"Oh, good. I was worried I gave you my friends'. She left it at my house the other day. I'm supposed to return it today."

She smiled and nodded.

"Do you have the time?" I asked.

She pointed to the clock on the wall behind her. "Looks like it's just after nine-fifteen."

"Right. Thanks."

It wasn't easy being this indecisive and irritating. If our roles were reversed, I would've kicked me out long ago. I admired her patience.

Once the transaction was completed, I picked up my coffee and pretended the cup slipped through my fingers. As it crashed to the floor, I gasped and cursed while the hot coffee splattered up on me and the counter. Based on the colorful language from the man behind me, he also got splashed.

"Oh, no!" I yelled. "Oh, my gosh. I'm so sorry!"

As I helped the barista clean up the mess, I hoped the stain would come out of my white sweatshirt.

But at least I had solidified my alibi.

CHAPTER 5

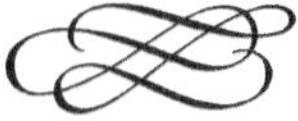

AFTER CLEANING the mess and buying a cappuccino for the man behind me in line, I returned to the hospital with two coffees, figuring Trevor would appreciate my trip.

As I walked down the hall toward Jacob's room, I heard yelling. I took a deep breath and prayed that my son and Vic had escaped undetected.

"Where have you been?" Mallory screeched at me as I entered the room. Trevor and Colin Breckshire were also present. "And where is my murder suspect?!"

Instead of screaming right back at her, I walked over to Trevor and handed him the coffee. "What are you talking about?" I asked, then glanced past them to the bed. "Where's my son?!" I set down my coffee. "Did you take him to jail?!"

Mallory seemed perplexed by my questioning. "N-no! I came to get him and he's not here!" She placed her hands on her gun belt and narrowed her gaze. "What did you do with him?"

"Do with him? What does that mean? Where... where is my son?" I met the gaze of everyone in the room. No one answered. "None of you know?"

Trevor put his hand on my shoulder. "We thought maybe you had something to do with his disappearance," he said softly.

"Now how would I do that?" I asked. "He was chained to the dang bed like a dog! Do I look like I can chew through metal?"

"Sometimes, yes," Mallory sneered.

"Where have you been?" Trevor asked, shooting her a glare.

Ignoring Mallory would be in my best interests. She was only trying to goad me and I wouldn't take the bait. "I went to get coffee," I said. Then I remembered he'd brought me one from the hospital not too long before I left. "The stuff here is awful, so since Jacob had gone back to sleep, I thought I'd slip out and get something from Cup of Go. It's already been a long day, and I needed some fresh air and good coffee."

"What's he doing here?" Mallory asked, pointing at Colin, who admittedly looked quite dapper in his grey suit and matching fedora.

"I called him," I replied. "You've accused my son of murdering a poor girl, and whether you think so or not, he deserves a defense."

Her cheeks reddened. "So you called him and then you left? That doesn't make any sense."

Colin cleared his throat. "If I may interject, I arrived here much quicker than I anticipated when I spoke to Ms. Dunner on the phone. If my appointment hadn't been canceled, I would've come later."

The old lawyer hadn't said anything about an appointment when we talked, so I appreciated his quick thinking. I hadn't given any consideration to the time between my phone call with him and his arrival, which would be an important detail for Mallory. Because why would I call an attorney, then leave when I was expecting him?

"I don't believe any of this," Mallory snarled.

"That's okay," I shot back. "I don't believe

half the stuff that comes out of your mouth, either."

She narrowed her gaze. "Maybe we should go down to the station and discuss what you've done with your son."

"I don't think that's necessary," Colin said. "It's apparent that Ms. Dunner has had a very difficult morning, and now to top it off, her son is missing."

Suddenly, all the stress boiled up within me and tears started falling. The last thing I wanted was to cry in front of Mallory, but I couldn't hold them back. "He's right. You've accused my son of murder, cuffed him to a bed, and all I wanted was a decent cup of coffee. My nerves are so shot, I dropped my latte and stained my white sweatshirt." I held the still damp clothing from my body. "Then I came back here only to find my son is missing." Trevor handed me a tissue as I swiped at my tears. "This has been a horrible day."

And I meant every word. The total breakdown that sat just on my peripheral vision began closing in. I took a deep breath and fought it. Collapsing under the weight of my anxiety and worry over Jacob's future wouldn't do him any good.

At that moment, all I wanted was my dog.

"I have no idea where my son is," I said, meeting Mallory's gaze.

"I'm going to check with Cup of Go and see that you were really there," she hissed.

"That's fine." I pointed to my cup I'd set down when I first arrived, then to the one Trevor held in his hand. "If that isn't enough evidence for you, then please, conduct your due diligence on this big mystery. And after that's done, find the real killer because I can promise you, it's not my kid."

With that, I marched out of the room and down the hallway. A few steps later, I remembered Trevor had driven me. Dang it! So much for my grand exit. But then I recalled Ava's friend, Bianca, had also been drugged and was behind one of the doors...

Names had been written on a white board outside each room. I discovered hers quickly and slipped in. Thankfully, I found her alone because I had no idea what I would have said if she'd been with family.

"Hi, Bianca," I said. "I'm Gina. My son was at the party with you last night."

Her long blonde hair sat in tangles around her shoulders. Red-rimmed eyes indicated she'd been crying.

"Who's your son?"

"Jacob Dunner."

She nodded. "He's very nice. Is he here, too?"

"Yes. I'm really sorry about Ava."

Tears welled in her eyes and tracked down her cheeks. "Me, too."

Realizing she had no idea Jacob was the suspect in her friends' killing, I walked over to the bed. "I was wondering if I could talk to you for a minute about what happened?"

"I already told the police everything I know."

"I'm sure you did. But I'm Jacob's mom, and I'm scared, Bianca. Who would drug the four of you?"

She shook her head. "I don't know."

"My son said that someone gave him water, then he didn't remember anything after that."

"That was my experience, too."

"Do you recall who gave you the bottle?" Jacob had mentioned someone named Terry, but he hadn't seemed very sure of it himself. I needed Bianca's version of events.

"Terry Burnell was the one who brought out the waters." She shook her head. "She's such a snot."

"Why is that?" I asked.

"She's always been after Ava's boyfriend,

Oliver. I guess now she can make her move. Why she'd want him, I don't know."

Bile rose in my throat. Had Terry drugged Ava, then killed her, and was now after her boyfriend? Could it be that simple, that childish?

Bianca apparently wasn't a fan of Oliver. "You don't like him," I said gently.

She crossed her arms over her chest. "I think he was cheating on Ava, but I couldn't prove it."

"What gave you that idea?"

"Just different things," she replied, shrugging. "I heard him on a phone call saying sweet nothings to someone, but it wasn't Ava because she was in class."

"Maybe she skipped?"

"No. Not Ava. Did you know she had perfect attendance from kindergarten through high school? *Perfect*. She even got an award at graduation for being the only one in our school district who never missed a day. It wasn't in her makeup to skip. Besides, that day I heard Oliver, it was a test day for her, so I *know* she was in school. She came back to the dorm and claimed she'd received an A. She wasn't taking calls from Oliver during her test."

"What else has Oliver done that made you think he was cheating on Ava?"

"We have English together and he sits in front of me. He was texting someone and I read it over his shoulder. They were making plans for dinner. At first I assumed it was Ava, but when she was home at that time, I mentioned that I thought she and Oliver were going out. She said they didn't have any plans because Oliver had a group project meeting he needed to attend."

"Do you think he was seeing Terry on the side?" I asked.

She shrugged. "I have no idea."

"Did you ever mention anything to Ava about him?"

"No."

"Why not, Bianca? It would seem like something you'd do if you cared about her."

"Because Ava wasn't exactly a saint either," she snapped. "She was cheating on Oliver with Gabriel."

Ah... the plot thickens. The rumors had been true.

"I just decided to keep my nose out of it." She sighed and laid her head back on the pillow. "But maybe I shouldn't have. Maybe then she'd still be alive."

We sat in silence for a long moment, then I asked, "Who do you think killed her?"

"My guess would be Gabriel. She'd broken it off with him after deciding Oliver was the one for her. She decided she'd made a mistake by getting involved with him. He'd left a couple of nasty voicemails, telling her she'd regret her decision."

I really wished I had a pen and pencil so I could jot down notes. Instead, I attempted to commit everything to memory.

"Like a threat?" I asked.

"I don't know. Maybe? I didn't see them."

Had Gabriel killed Ava because she'd chosen Oliver?

"But you said Terry brought out the waters," I said. "How does that correlate with Gabriel killing her?"

"I don't know," she huffed. "Now that you say it though, it doesn't make sense."

"It's my understanding that Gabriel was at the party last night. Did he stay long?"

"Yeah, he showed up. I couldn't believe it. I'm not sure how long he stayed. I wasn't paying attention. The guy's a slimeball to do that."

"Did he and Oliver have words?"

"Oh, yes. Unfortunately, that's when

Gabriel let Oliver know Ava had been cheating on him. Oliver was furious."

This young adult drama kept getting more and more interesting. "So, just to clarify, Oliver was upset with Ava for cheating, even though he'd been seeing someone behind her back."

"Yes. Total double standard if you ask me." She sighed and shook her head. "I hate men. I'm never going to get married."

Instead of launching into a lecture on how if you find the right man life could be very good, I said, "And Gabriel was upset with Ava because she'd broken it off with him."

"Exactly. She was like the center of a tornado. She sucked up everything and everyone around her and then spit out whoever she didn't want to keep."

Jacob had referred to Ava in a similar way, calling her the 'center of everything.' He'd never been in her inner circle, but Bianca had. Perhaps Ava had spit her out and she'd killed her out of spite?

But that didn't make any sense because Bianca had been drugged. She wouldn't have been able to wrap a rope around her friend's neck.

It all came back to Terry, the one who had

brought the water. I was going to track her down and wring the truth out of her.

"Thanks for your time, Bianca." I said. "Hopefully, you'll be out of here soon."

"I hope so, too. I hate it here."

After giving her hand a quick squeeze, I glanced out into the hallway before slipping out the door. The hum of voices indicated the emergency clinic was still quite busy, but the hallway was clear. Right across from Bianca's room was Eric's. I peeked in to find him with his parents. He was awake and talking, so I assumed he'd be leaving the emergency clinic at any time.

As I rounded the corner toward the backside of the building, I was relieved to find the service door open.

I'd escaped.

And now I needed to find a killer.

CHAPTER 6

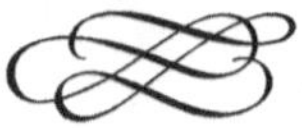

I HURRIED past the dumpster and decided to take the back streets home. When I arrived, I wouldn't be surprised to find Trevor waiting for me. I'd deal with that later. For now, I had a bunch of kids who'd found themselves in a very bad situation and one had died.

Jacob wasn't going to take the fall for it, though.

Suddenly, I heard little cries. As I turned slowly, they sounded again. "What the heck?" I whispered. The sounds were coming from the dumpster. I dropped to my hands and knees and looked under it, then walked around it. I waited.

When they sounded again, I realized the noise was coming from inside the dumpster.

Cursing, I flipped open the top and hauled my-self up to the rim. Below me, a puppy stared up at me, its big brown eyes pleading for help.

Someone had put a puppy in a dumpster.

I swore some more. There wasn't any garbage surrounding the ball of blonde fluff, so this had happened very recently.

"Hello, my little friend," I said gently. "Who did this to you?"

More cries. I didn't have time to waste, so I dropped to the inside with a loud thud. Thankfully, my wild childhood had taught me how to climb all sorts of fences. I'd been in and out of a few dumpsters in my time as well.

My new friend barked twice, then slowly came toward me as I crouched down. "Hey, there," I said softly. "What do you say we get you out of here?"

The little tongue licked my fingers, so I took it as a "yes." I grabbed the puppy and held it to my chest, quickly checking for a sex. "Well, little girl, you're stuck with me. I'm not sure if that's a good thing for you right now, but it's better than being in here."

Even though my sweatshirt was still slightly damp from the coffee, I tucked it into my jeans and gently placed the puppy inside. Before she could squirm too much and dislodge my makeshift baby carrier, I scrambled up the side of the dumpster. Once on top, I straddled it, then pulled her out. My knees and ankles whimpered when I jumped to the ground. "That was a lot easier to take when I was twelve," I muttered.

She licked my cheek, her blonde tail thumping against my ribs. "You are cute as heck," I said, stroking her little head. I figured she was probably about two to three months old.

As I walked home, she settled in my arms and seemed perfectly content. The last thing I needed was a puppy, especially with Jacob being accused of murder. I had to find out who really killed Ava, and caring for a puppy didn't allow for a lot of free time. And then there was the fact that Daisy hated puppies... well, she said she did, anyway. When we'd had that whole litter at Christmastime, she'd had fun with them while complaining.

"I guess we'll just have to see what happens," I said. "My son is in a lot of trouble and I need to help him." She licked my face again. "If you keep being this cute, we're going to get along just fine."

My new charge and I walked the rest of the way home in silence. Once again, I wished I had a pen and paper. There were so many thoughts swirling in my head, I needed to jot them down.

I had been right. When I arrived home, Trevor's truck sat in my driveway. Taking a deep breath, I steeled myself for his anger. He had to know I was behind Jacob's disappearance. If he didn't, he wasn't as smart as I thought he was.

I approached the rear of his vehicle and he exited. "Where is he, Gina? And why are you carrying a puppy?"

"I swear to you, I don't know where Jacob is," I replied. "And I found this little one in the dumpster. I'd like to tie a rope around the neck of whoever did this and pull tightly."

Trevor winced. "Kind of a bad choice of words there, Dunner."

Right. That's exactly how Ava had died. A bad choice of words, indeed. "Sorry about that. Do you want to come in?"

He sighed and shook his head. "Sure."

I grinned, pleased he wasn't *that* angry with me.

"Speaking of ropes, did you find out anything about the one around Ava's neck?"

"Nope. It looks like it came from their

boat. Every boat in the area will most likely have one. It's nothing special."

I didn't know what I was hoping for. Maybe some unique rope only used in a certain profession that would narrow down our list of suspects.

As I unlocked the door, he said, "Quick change of subject... I know you've told me you don't want to know anything about your mother—"

"Stop right there. She's the last thing I can think about. I'm focused solely on Jacob, Trevor."

He mumbled something about how sorry I'd be, but I ignored him as Daisy started yelling from inside. "Gina! Gina! You're home! It's been forever! I missed you!"

I opened the door and her tail stopped wagging almost immediately. "Who is that?!" she screeched. "You went to help Jacob and you brought home a *puppy*? How does that work, Gina?! You're *cheating* on me!"

Reaching down, I stroked her head. "Smell the puppy, Daisy. She's going to be staying with us for a while."

"I hate puppies," she muttered as she buried her nose in puppy fur. When she received a lick on the tip of her nose, Daisy giggled. "Okay, maybe this one isn't too bad. Put her down."

After I set her on the floor, Daisy did a full nose-to-tail exploration. "She's cute, Gina. Almost as cute as me."

"Maybe you two can be friends," I suggested. "She needs everyone to be nice to her."

Trevor chuckled behind me. "She can't understand a word you're saying to her, Gina."

If only he knew. If only I was brave enough to tell him the truth. I stood and smiled. "I can hope she does. Let me get the little one some food."

Everyone followed me into the kitchen.

"If you're going to feed her, it's only fair that you feed me, too, Gina." Daisy sat at my feet. "I've been a very good dog since you left this morning. And you didn't feed me."

My departure had been quite hasty, so I prepared two bowls, set them down, and then leaned against the counter to monitor them. To my surprise, both dogs stuck to their own bowls.

"Who throws a puppy in a dumpster?" Trevor asked.

"I don't know," I muttered. "And it's probably best that I don't." My visceral reaction to animal cruelty bordered on violence. I had actually broken a man's nose during a rescue once a few years back. He hadn't pressed charges against me because he was up to his bloody nostrils in indictments for the animals and other shady activities.

"She's cute, though," he said. "A little puff of blonde."

"Yes. Probably a lab, or maybe a retriever."

Once she finished with her meal, she began yapping at Daisy. When she didn't get a response, she nipped at her foot.

Daisy growled.

"Hey!" I yelled. "No growling!"

"I told her to let me finish my food, and then I'd play with her!" Daisy retorted. She then placed her paw on the little blonde head and pressed until the puppy was flat on her stomach. "She needs to learn some manners."

Trevor laughed as Daisy held her head down.

I sighed and looked at him. Now that I was certain Daisy wouldn't hurt our newest rescue, I felt confident changing my focus. "Let's sit down and figure out who murdered Ava."

Trevor plopped down on a chair at a kitchen table. "I'm exhausted."

I was too, but I couldn't rest until I found the killer. After starting a pot of coffee, I grabbed my notebook and pen from a drawer, then took a seat across from him. "Okay, so let's start at the beginning. Who were the last kids at the party? I have Jacob, Eric, Ava, Oliver, Terry and Bianca for sure." I wrote down their names. "Now it seems that people are unsure if Gabriel was there or not when Terry served the water."

"The four kids I talked to at the emergency clinic weren't certain," Trevor replied. When the coffee pot sputtered, notifying us it was done brewing, he stood and pulled two cups from the cupboard, then poured us each a coffee. "But when I spoke to Gabriel at the scene, he said he'd left, but come back to find Ava dead and everyone asleep. He's the one who called 9-1-1."

"Did you believe him?" I asked, jotting down the information.

"I didn't see a reason not to. He was really upset." Trevor set the coffee down in front of me, then took his seat. "And don't forget Zoe. She was there when I arrived and said she'd been sleeping."

Next to Jacob, Eric, Ava, and Bianca, I wrote *drugged*.

"What about Oliver? I asked.

"He was hard to wake, but he said he'd had a lot to drink."

"So, Oliver, Ava's boyfriend, was drunk. Zoe fell asleep. Gabriel left and came back." I tapped my pen against the paper. "And where was Terry?"

"When I arrived at the Willard home this morning, Terry wasn't there."

I arched an eyebrow and picked up my coffee. "So she drugged everyone, killed Ava and... took off?"

"Would you hang around if you'd murdered someone?"

Good point.

"We aren't sure if Oliver and Terry were dating on the side, are we?" I asked.

He shook his head. "No, but I think anything is a possibility at this point. Could she have killed off Ava to have a chance with Oliver?"

"I'd never do something like that, but I suppose so. Where does Terry live?"

"She's about twenty minutes outside of town," he said. "I just got notification of her address when you walked up."

I took another sip of coffee, some of it dribbling down my chin to my sweatshirt. I glanced down at the stain.

"I was going to tell you to be careful with that so you don't stain your sweatshirt, but then I remembered you already had."

"Thanks," I muttered. "Let me go change."

As I hurried down the hall, Daisy ran past me with our little friend at her heels and into the bedroom. I shut the door behind me so I could have a quick conversation with my dog.

Daisy jumped on the bed, but the puppy couldn't quite make it. As it whined and tried to follow Daisy, my dog stood at the edge and stared down at her. "Come on, you little turd! You can do it! Gina, tell her she can do it!"

I picked up the blond fluffball and set her on the bed, then pulled off my sweatshirt. "What do you want to name her?"

"I get to name her?" Daisy asked.

"Yes." I pulled out a sweatshirt from my drawer, slipped it on, then sat on the bed. "I'm going to need your help over the next couple of weeks."

"What do you need me to do?" Daisy sat down next to me. She wagged her tail while the puppy chased it.

"Exactly what you're doing. Take care of her."

"I can do that," she said. "I kind of like her a little bit. I'm glad you found her."

"Did she tell you *where* I found her?"

"Yes. She said a bad man put her in the garbage and she was really scared."

"I'm happy I was there to fish her out." I shook my head, trying to contain my rage. "I really hate people sometimes."

"What's going on with Jacob?" Daisy asked.

"He's gone," I whispered in case Trevor had come down the hall. "I don't know where, but he's safe."

"So what happens next?"

"Well, Trevor thinks I had something to do with his disappearance, so I'm hopeful that he allows me access to the case information, but if he doesn't, I wouldn't be surprised."

Daisy giggled. "Gina, Jacob's your son. Of course you made him disappear." She kept moving her tail, and the puppy continued to chase it.

"Will you help me out these next couple of weeks?"

"Yeppers! I'll be a very good dog and keep this little brat in line."

"Thank you," I sighed. I grabbed the sides

of her face and kissed her nose. "You're the best dog ever."

Daisy licked my cheek. "I'm going to remind you about saying this when you find the chewed-up sock in the bathroom."

CHAPTER 7

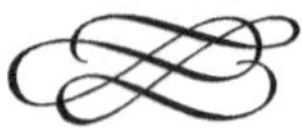

I WAS TOO tired to be mad. Instead, I walked into the bathroom, found the mangled sock, and tossed it in the trash.

"You didn't feed me before you left, so I was hungry," Daisy called while she wrestled with the puppy. "And I think I'm going to name her Mustard."

Mustard? I hurried back to the bathroom. "Why in the world would you name a puppy Mustard?"

Daisy glanced up at me, then returned to her playing. "Because she's yellow. And that way I can call her Musty and she'll answer. It'll be super cute!"

"What about Goldie or Sunny?"

"What about Twinkie or Cornbread?"

"I'm seeing a pattern here," I muttered. "That's okay, we'll call her Mustard."

"Yay!" She took the puppy's head in her mouth. "Look, Mustard! I can fit your head in my mouth!"

A knock sounded at the bedroom door. "Gina?" Trevor called. "I need to head out to go talk to Terry. Are you coming?"

"He's not that mad at you," Daisy said. "Go with Trevor. Mustard and I will be good doggies."

I gave them both a quick kiss, then opened the door. "Yes, I'm going with you. I appreciate you taking me."

"I was only going to take you if you gave me Jacob's location," he replied, crossing his arms over his chest. "But I couldn't do that to you."

Throwing my hands in the air, I said, "Trevor, I honestly don't know where he is. When I left to get coffee, he was sleeping. When I got back, he was gone."

"Mallory's on a mission to prove you interfered with an investigation."

I shrugged. "I don't know what to tell her, or you. I didn't do anything."

"Did you make any calls before you went to get coffee?"

I almost lied, but Mallory probably already had my phone records. If not, they'd be in her hands shortly. "Yes. I called Vic to let him know his nephew was in the hospital."

"Do you think Vic may have taken him?"

I shrugged. "That would be pretty bold of him to saunter into the emergency clinic, break the handcuffs, then walk out the front door with Jacob."

Trevor narrowed his gaze. "You're right. Even Vic isn't that stupid."

I brushed past him and walked down the hall toward the front door. "Let's go see Terry."

We rode in silence and I had the distinct feeling Trevor was trying to decipher just how deep my lies ran. I kept my mouth shut and my eyes on the road.

Jacob's disappearing act had put Trevor in a difficult position. With us dating, of course he didn't want Jacob to be hit with charges on a crime he didn't commit. But at the same time, he had a job to do, and his boss said my son was guilty. He walked a fine line of trying to please both me and Mallory. Yes, I had sympathy for him, but I wouldn't play by her rules or deviate from my plan of finding the killer. She would *not* sink her claws into my son.

"I feel like I'm in between a rock and a hard

place," Trevor said. Apparently, his thoughts had mirrored mine. "I'd hoped the circumstances would be different when I finally had the guts to say this to you, but I love you, Gina. I'm not going to let Jacob go to jail for this killing. I'll do whatever's necessary to find the real murderer."

Love? He loved *me*? Yes, we'd been spending as much time together as possible, but the L-word hadn't come into play. Frankly, I wasn't sure how I felt about the statement. My heart had skipped a couple of beats and my stomach clenched. I cared deeply for Trevor, but was I in love? Would I even know if I was? And how did I respond?

"Thanks, Trevor," I said, laying my hand over his. "I'm glad to know you're on my side."

He squeezed my fingers and at that point, I knew we were going to get to the end of the horrible tragedy relatively emotionally unscathed.

"It's down this street here," Trevor said. We turned right and he recited the address. I noticed the house just as his phone announced we'd arrived.

The tidy brown home with white trim stood behind a swath of green grass. Daffodils and petunias lined the walkway to the front door. A pickup truck stood in the driveway, so I hoped that indicated someone was home.

"Cute place," Trevor murmured.

I nodded and stepped from the car while admiring all the pretty flowers. I didn't have much of a green thumb, although I did try. Every now and then I'd buy something, plant it, baby it, and watch it slowly perish.

We walked up the path to the door and Trevor knocked. I took a deep breath and hoped we could nail Terry to the wall. I imagined her opening the door, confessing, and this whole mess being over. Unfortunately, I had a feeling it wouldn't be that easy.

A man in his fifties answered. Big and strong with a head of gray hair and a heavily lined face, I guessed he'd made his living working outside.

"We're here to see Terry Burnell," Trevor said, flashing his badge.

He furrowed his brow in confusion. "For what?"

"She attended a party last night, and we have some questions."

"What kind of questions?" he asked.

Trevor sighed. "Like I said, sir, she was at a party. It's about the party."

"I'm her father, deputy. Is my girl in trouble?"

"We aren't sure," I interjected. "That's why we want to ask her questions."

I fully understood Mr. Burnell's hesitation at fetching his daughter. He wanted to protect her, just as I was doing with Jacob.

"Does she need a lawyer?" he asked.

"That's up to you, sir," Trevor replied. "At this time, I'd say the answer is no."

Seemingly satisfied, he nodded and stepped to the side. I followed Trevor in. Mr. Burnell shut the door and moved past us. "Come on in here," he said.

He led us into the kitchen and pointed at the table. "Have a seat. I'll get her."

I glanced around as I sat down. Someone was very fond of roosters. The cookie jar, the door-knobs and the wallpaper bordering—all roosters.

A moment later, Mr. Burnell appeared from the hallway, his daughter in tow. Based on the way she rubbed her eyes and the white and pink robe she wore, she'd been sleeping.

Probably needed a nap after a night of drugging people.

Trevor stood. "Hi, Terry. I'm Deputy Trevor Hutchinson. I need to ask you some questions about the party at the Willard place last night."

She sat down across from me. Stringy blond hair framed her round face to her chin. Her red-rimmed gaze met mine, but quickly found its way to the tabletop. I couldn't tell if she was a bit plump, or if the robe was just really fluffy.

"What about it?" she mumbled as her father laid his hand on her shoulder, then sat down next to her. Trevor took his place by me. "I'm really tired."

"So you got home late last night?" Trevor asked.

She nodded, her gaze still firmly set on the tiled table. Not surprisingly, each tile held a picture of a rooster.

"Can you tell us what happened at the party? Anything big?"

"Like what?" She glanced up at him.

"Did you argue with anyone?" Trevor questioned. "Or did anyone start something with you?"

She shook her head.

"Did you know that Ava Willard is dead?" I asked gently.

Her eyes welled. "Yes. It's all over Snapchat."

"What the heck?!" her father boomed. "Someone died at the party? Was it drugs?!"

Terry flinched and wiped her cheeks.

"There were drugs involved, right, Terry?" I prodded.

"What happened last night?" Trevor asked.

"Nothing!" Terry wailed. "I don't know anything!"

"I think you do," I replied. "We have four people who say that you gave them a bottle of water, and then they don't remember anything else about the night. Did you intentionally drug them?"

"My daughter was involved?" Mr. Burnell yelled. His face had turned a shade of red reserved for tomatoes and cherries. I worried he was having a stroke.

The room went quiet until Terry began sniffing. "I didn't mean to," she whispered. "It was only supposed to be Ava."

I traded glances with Trevor. "Can you explain what happened?"

She finally met my gaze. Anger gleamed in her eyes "Ava was outside with Bianca and two boys. Her boyfriend, Oliver, was passed out in the house. I wanted to talk to him, but I didn't want Ava to walk in."

"So... you drugged her?" The two boys she referred to must have been Jacob and Eric.

"Yes. I roofied her," she spat.

"You gave another girl a date rape drug?" her father asked incredulously. He then turned his gaze to the ceiling. "Lord have mercy. Give me strength."

"And why did you want to drug Ava?"

"I just told you. I wanted to talk to Oliver, and I didn't want her walking in on us."

Confused, I stared at her a long moment. Why would she care if Ava walked in while she was talking to her boyfriend? Unless... unless Terry had other plans besides a simple chat.

"Do you have a bit of a crush on Oliver?" I asked.

She nodded, her gaze returning to the tabletop.

Trevor cleared his throat. "What did you want to talk with him about?"

"About how Ava was cheating on him," Terry replied quietly. "About how he deserved a better girlfriend."

"Is that girlfriend you?"

She didn't answer, but I knew Trevor had nailed it. Terry wanted Oliver for herself. If she was willing to drug his girlfriend, did she have the gumption to kill her as well?

But if Terry only wanted to silence Ava for a bit while she made the moves on her boyfriend, how did three other people end up drugged?

After I voiced my question, she rolled her eyes. "I brought out the waters and they started playing this stupid game where they threw them up in the air. Everyone ended up drinking everyone else's water."

"Did you try to stop them?" Trevor asked.

"What was I supposed to say?" she retorted. "I only want to drug Ava so quit drinking her water?"

Her father placed his elbows on the table and rested his head in his hands. "Good God," he muttered. "Please forgive her."

"What happened when you realized that everyone was going to be drugged?" I asked.

"I left." She shrugged.

"Are you sure, Terry?" I leaned forward and placed my hands over hers on top of the table. "Are you sure you came home and you didn't take measures to get Ava permanently out of the way?"

"I didn't kill her," she grumbled. "I came home when I realized what was going to happen."

"We'll be able to track your movements via your phone," Trevor stated.

Her father shot to his feet. "And on that note, I'm going to have to ask you to leave. I think we need a lawyer."

I ignored him. "Where did you get the drugs, Terry?"

"Some guy was selling them outside Hold Your Horses."

Ah, yes. The shady bar on the outskirts of town. Not a nice place to be, and certainly not appropriate for a young woman such as Terry.

"What did you buy?" I asked.

"Please leave!" Mr. Burnell yelled. "Terry and I need to speak to a lawyer, and then she needs to pray and repent for her sins."

Trevor nudged me, giving me the cue that the conversation had ended. Terry's father escorted us to the door in silence and watched us walk down the pathway to Trevor's vehicle. Once we were in his truck, Trevor pulled away from the curb.

"What do you think?" he asked.

I shrugged and shook my head. "If she admits to the drugging, I don't see murder as that big of a leap."

CHAPTER 8

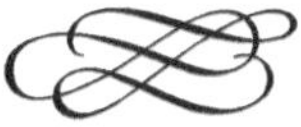

"So what's next?" I asked as soon as we were inside his truck. "Who are we interviewing?"

"Right now, I think it's a good idea to have some downtime," he said. "It's been a long day, and I know I'm exhausted."

"So am I," I grumbled. "But I have to find out who killed Ava."

"We will, Gina," he assured, taking my hand in his. "We will. But we also need to be rested to do so or we'll just be going around in circles and not thinking properly."

I nodded, hating that he was right. For now, Jacob was safe. I didn't know where, but at least he wasn't in Mallory's clutches.

"I'd like to take a look at the crime scene," I said.

He shook his head. "No can do. I can send you some pictures, but the house is locked up. Even the Willards aren't allowed in right now."

"Where does Ava's boyfriend, Oliver, live?" I asked.

"He's from around here. We can go see him tomorrow, after you rest."

"Do you think he could've killed her?"

He shrugged. "I don't see why not. He'd found out Ava was also seeing Gabriel. Maybe he snapped while he was drunk."

"Do you think he could've done it and not even remember?"

"I don't know." Trevor shook his head. "I can't imagine blacking out and killing someone. That's hardcore. Besides, if he was as drunk as everyone says, I'd think he'd be pretty easy to fight off."

"I suppose you're right," I muttered. "But I do want to meet with Oliver, so don't go there without me, okay?"

"Yes, ma'am."

I glanced out the window and realized we were quite close to my house. "Are you taking me home?"

"Remember that resting thing we discussed? You're going to do that."

As we rounded the corner to my street, I was about to invite him in. Then I noticed my father's car in the driveway.

"What's he doing here?" I asked. Not that I expected Trevor to have an answer. When he pulled into the driveway, I found my father sitting on the porch swing with a woman.

"Who is that?" I asked. "And why is he bringing her to my house?"

"Oh, boy," Trevor muttered.

I turned to him, then glanced back at the woman. Long gray hair hung around her slim shoulders. My father waved at me and the woman stood, then crossed her arms over her chest. We were built similarly in stature. After pushing my glasses up my nose, I squinted at her. She seemed familiar.

The reality gut-punched me. "Drive away," I ordered. "Drive away now!"

"Gina, that's your mom."

"I know that!" I yelled. Panic clawed at my throat. "Why didn't you tell me she was coming to town?!"

"I tried," he said, his voice calm.

"You said she was in prison!"

"Yes, I did. And now she's out, standing on

your porch. I tried to tell you just the other day she was on her way and you didn't want to hear it."

I swore and fisted my hands in my lap.

"I'm sorry this is such a big surprise for you, Gina." He gently squeezed my hand. "You're going to have to face this."

Tears welled in my eyes as I stared at her. "Not now. Not with Jacob in trouble."

"Unless you're going to disappear to where you've hidden Jacob, I don't think you have a choice."

Actually, that was an excellent idea. But I wouldn't be able to investigate his case if I was in hiding.

Trevor was right. I needed to face this head on.

As I opened the door, I felt like a child who'd done something terrible and was now going to face the consequences.

You are closer to fifty than forty. She left you. You've done nothing wrong.

I squared my shoulders and marched up to them with Trevor trailing behind me. My dad stood and smiled.

"Hi, Gina," he said. "This is—"

"She knows exactly who I am," Brandy Dunner said. "I can see it in her eyes."

"You've shown up at a really bad time," I replied, meeting her gaze. "My son is in trouble."

"We heard," my dad said. He walked over and kissed my cheek. "Can we have a minute of your time?"

Daisy peered through the living room window. "Gina! Gina!" she yelled. "Mustard has to pee! Hurry! Come inside!"

With a sigh, I quickly retrieved my keys and opened the front door. Daisy ran for the kitchen with Mustard on her heels. Just as I unlocked the back door, Mustard relieved herself on the tile then began to whine.

"That's okay, little one," Daisy said. "Let's go outside. Gina will clean that up."

The two dogs hurried into the yard while I stared at the pee. Could this day get any worse? Not that I blamed the puppy for the accident. Clean up would be quick. But it seemed like a very insignificant happening that layered on to a bunch of very significant occurrences, and I was close to my breaking point. What that would look like, I had no idea. Tears? Probably not. Me saying a bunch of stuff I'd regret later? Most likely.

I didn't have the bandwidth to deal with my mother. Sure, I had plenty of questions, but at that moment, I needed to concentrate on Jacob.

After gathering my paper towels and cleaner, I wiped up Mustard's mess. I listened as Trevor played the host in my living room. I knew he was tired as well, but I really appreciated him acting as a barrier.

"Do you need some help?"

I glanced up to find my mother leaning against the doorway.

"No." I sighed and sprayed the floor again, then ripped off a few more paper towels.

"I felt it was best I didn't contact you," she said. "At first, it was to keep you safe. Then, I got into some trouble and figured you didn't need to know about it."

"I can't do this right now," I said. It took every ounce of energy I had to stand and meet her gaze. "Maybe some other time when my son isn't in trouble."

She nodded. "Understood, Gina." Her gaze raked over me from head-to-toe. "You look good. Your dad tells me you're a dog rescuer."

"Among other things."

She smiled. "He said you were always busy and hated being idle."

I nodded.

"Just like me," she whispered, then gave me

a wink. "I'll get out of your hair, but I hope we can talk sometime soon."

My ability to sidestep this difficult situation and ignore it had come to an end. "Okay. I'll let you know."

"If you need any help, I'm at your father's."

She returned to the living room, and I stared at the floor. I had no idea what she could possibly do to help me.

I lifted my gaze when my father entered. "I'll see you later, Gina."

"I don't want her here," I hissed. "When did she come back?"

He glanced over his shoulder, then turned to me. "She showed up yesterday," he whispered. "I knew she was coming, though."

"Has Vic seen her?"

"Yes. Earlier today. She also met Jacob."

I narrowed my gaze, wondering what Jacob thought of his newly acquired grandmother. "She's not going to rat on him for favors with the law, is she? If she does, I'll make her life so miserable, she'll be begging to go back to prison."

Theo Dunner threw his head back and laughed. "I know you will, but no way, baby. No way. She'd never do anything like that. Do what you need to get done, but be careful with Trevor. He is the law, and you're breaking it."

"I will."

"I also wanted to give you this." He pulled a small burner phone that could be found at any store from his pocket. "When that rings, it's Vic and Jacob. Vic doesn't want you using your regular line to contact him."

After taking the device, I stared at it a long while. It felt like a lifeline to my son, and suddenly, I was at peace with Jacob being with Vic, and even felt a bit better about Brandy showing up. "Thanks, Dad."

"Come here and give your old man a hug."

For a long moment, I closed my eyes while my father embraced me. In some ways, it revitalized me. He had my back. "Call us if you need anything," he said. "We may be old, but both your mom and I are quite resourceful. We're your family, Gina, and we'll do whatever it takes for you to clear Jacob."

"Thanks." Again, I had no idea what they could do that I couldn't, but I appreciated the sentiment, even if it sounded like something out of a mob movie.

I followed him to the living room. He shook Trevor's hand, and then my parents left.

Trevor turned to me as I let out an audible sigh. "You okay?"

"Yes. Great. Fricking fantastic." My attempt at hiding my sarcasm had failed.

Daisy barked at the back door and I hurried to open it for her and Mustard. Both of them flew past me and scurried down the hall. Mustard was so fluffy, it was hard to see her legs. At least Daisy had taken a liking to the unscheduled rescue. Not everything that had happened in the past twenty-four hours had been terrible.

"Dang cute puppy," Trevor said, chuckling. "Why don't you sit down? I'll get us each a glass of wine."

I wouldn't argue with that stellar idea. As I plopped down on the cushions, I tried to calm my nerves. Jacob was safe for now. I'd find the real killer if it was the last thing I did, and I'd break laws to do so. Heck, I already had by busting my kid out of the emergency clinic.

As promised, Trevor came in with two glasses of wine. We sat in silence as I slowly sipped the red liquid. The stress in my shoulders faded and I took a few deep breaths.

"Do you want to know about your mom?" he asked.

I had to admit, I was somewhat curious, but I had to focus on Jacob.

"She's quite the character," he continued.

My curiosity had been piqued. Maybe it would be good to think about something besides my son for a few minutes. Sometimes, placing my attention on another topic offered me clarity. In this case, perhaps after I was done listening to Trevor, I'd have figured out who killed Ava.

"Okay." I sighed. "Let's hear it. What has the illustrious Brandy Dunner been doing since she walked out on her family all those years ago?"

Trevor set down his glass. "I've spent hours researching her. She's had a pretty interesting journey."

"Okay, so tell me."

"Have you ever heard of New York's Notorious Nanny?"

CHAPTER 9

I FURROWED MY BROW. "No. Is she that person?"

"Yep. One and the same. We later found out she operated throughout the eastern seaboard for decades."

"What did she do?" I asked.

"Well, as the moniker indicates, she was a nanny."

I stared at Trevor for a long moment. "And being a nanny led her to going to prison... how? I'm not sure I want to know, especially if she was doing something to the kids."

"No, no," Trevor assured me. "Nothing like that."

Relief washed through me. At least my

mother wasn't a pedophile. "Then what did she do?"

"After leaving here, she was in and out of jail around the west coast for about a decade. Stupid stuff like petty theft. Then, she went east. Somewhere along the way, she changed her name to Trinity Roberts, concocted a very detailed resume of her previous nanny jobs on the west coast, and began applying for jobs."

Trinity Roberts, aka, Brandy Dunner, worked for one influential New York family for almost a decade caring for the couple's two children.

"When the daughter turned fifteen and the boy was thirteen, the parents decided to send their kids to a European boarding school," Trevor continued. "And the children were not happy about it, which upset Trinity. She had grown very attached to her charges, and to make things worse, she was going to be out of a job, one she liked very much and had given her stability for years."

The time came to ship the kids off, and Trinity was let go. She may have been able to walk away, but they withheld her last paycheck, saying the kids were old enough and didn't need her anyway.

"So she was out of a place to live and had

been shorted money," I said, now thoroughly enthralled with the story of the woman who raised other people's kids. "What happened then?"

Trevor shrugged. "She got her revenge. Police believe that was her first big job."

"What did she do?"

"Apparently, no one expected their long-term employee they'd shafted to rob them. They didn't change the alarm code and your mom was intimately familiar with their daily schedules. Every Sunday night, they'd open a safe in their library and pull out pocket-cash for the week. She'd been with them long enough to know that sometimes, the safe was locked after the money grab. Sometimes it wasn't. She sauntered into the house one Wednesday afternoon —the day she knew housekeeping was off— deactivated the alarm and walked into the library. The owner swore they'd locked the safe, but who knows? She made off with twenty-thousand dollars."

I almost choked on my wine. "Wow. That's... that's crazy. How come they never arrested her?"

"The cops were never sure it was her. In fact, they spent months trying to pin it on housekeeping. It wasn't until years later when they saw a pattern emerging from the heists that they realized this may have been her first."

"How many were there?" I asked.

"When she was finally caught, there were dozens that they could trace back to her, but between you and me, I think there were more. She only admitted to the ones where they had hard evidence."

"And how do you know all this about her?" I asked. "I thought you were just doing a bit of a background check."

"I did, and it led to some amazing rabbit holes. I was able to watch police interviews with her after they finally arrested her, read police reports and watch the trial. It was all pretty fascinating, so I spent my free time on it."

How many hours had he spent figuring out my mother's history? It sounded like far too many.

I shook my head. "How did she get away with that for so long?"

"She's resourceful," Trevor said. "After each job, she'd change her name and appearance, then move into a different area. I'm not sure how she managed all the reference and referrals she provided her employers, but she did."

Did I note a little admiration in his voice? "You're impressed with her."

"A bit," he replied. "She fooled a lot of people for a long time."

"She *stole* from people, Trevor," I reminded him.

"But see, that's the thing," he said. "Not everyone."

"What does that mean?"

"In the interview tapes I watched, she said she only stole from those who were mean to their kids."

"Mean to the kids?" I asked.

"She told the cops that a lot of her clientele were often too busy for their children, and your mom often took on the role of a mother figure for the kids. They confided in her, told her things they couldn't tell their parents, mainly because they were never around."

"That doesn't give her the right to steal, though."

He shrugged. "When her time with a family was over, she'd take from them. She said it was her way of getting back at them for the way they'd neglected their kids. She said she always tried to stay with a family as long as possible in order to offer the children stability. Unfortunately, according to Brandy, parents don't like it when the kids become too close to the help. Many times, that's when the nanny is cut loose."

"I don't see how robbing anyone changes anything," I muttered. "It doesn't make sense."

"We don't need to understand it, Gina," he said. "She felt they were awful parents, so she robbed them." He shrugged. "I guess she thought she'd hurt them in a very important place."

"Did she always steal cash?"

"Oh, no," he said. "Jewelry, paintings, bonds... you name it, she took it."

"I assume she fenced all of it?"

"Yes."

"What was the estimated total of her jobs?"

"No one had a really clear number because we don't know the extent of it all, but someone estimated in the hundreds of thousands based on the crimes they could directly pin on her," he said.

"That's a lot of money. She must've been living large."

"Not really," he replied. "When they finally caught up with her and arrested her in North Carolina, she was living in a small home. In the interviews, she said she donated most of the money to children's charities and only kept what she needed to survive."

"How strange."

"Yes, your mother is definitely an interesting character."

I couldn't help but wonder if her work with children and her donations to charities was her way of trying to erase guilt for leaving her own kids.

"Brandy has a special set of skills," Trevor continued. "She's an expert lockpicker. At one house, she scaled the side of a building to the upstairs balcony and let herself in while the parents were downstairs entertaining. She'd admitted to learning how to crack safes. She's strong, athletic and smart." He chuckled and shook his head. "I guess I do respect her."

I stared at him, almost disgusted that a cop would find a criminal so admirable.

"Don't look at me like that," he said, smiling. "I know what she did was wrong. I've just spent a lot of time watching video footage of interviews with her, and I was impressed." He placed his arm over my shoulder and pulled me close. "You come from some interesting people, Gina."

"I know," I said. With a sigh, I laid my head on him. "Master criminals, every single one of them. Hopefully, none of it rubs off on Jacob and he doesn't become the next prolific serial killer."

"Nah, he's a good kid with a great mom. No chance of that." We sat in silence for a long while.

"It's fascinating," he continued. "You have your father, who used to be a drug dealer, and your mother, a master burglar. Your brother has also been in trouble with the law but seems to have straightened himself out. Then there's you—someone who is hot on the trail of a murderer. Someone who has brought people to justice, time and time again. I guess in this case, two wrongs do make a right."

I never saw myself as a caped crusader. Instead, there had always been a reason for me to get involved in solving killings. Either there was someone who I cared deeply for accused, or Mallory was just being her usual idiot self and I needed to prove her wrong. The halo he'd placed on me wasn't deserved. My actions had always been self-serving.

"As long as Jacob doesn't get the urge to start dealing drugs or burglarizing rich people, I'll be happy."

"Do you want to tell me where he's at?"

I sighed and shut my eyes for a long moment. "Trevor, even if I knew, I wouldn't tell you. I'm sorry, but even though you're sitting here with me sharing my bottle of wine, you are still on the 'other' side."

"Fair enough," he said. "But at some point, you'll have to understand I'm on your side. That's the only side I want to be on, Gina."

I sat up and gave him a quick kiss on the cheek just as Daisy walked in. "Whew, I'm super tired," she said, jumping up on the couch and curling up next to me. "Watching a puppy is hard work."

Glancing down the hall, I wondered where Mustard had gone. "I hope the puppy is okay," I said, nudging her. With Trevor present, I couldn't ask her outright.

"Mustard's asleep," she replied. "I'm so tired, Gina. I think I may retire from my position."

Smiling, I stroked her head as her eyes closed. Seconds later, she was snoring softly.

I better get going," Trevor said. He leaned over and kissed me. "I've got an early morning, and then we'll head over and talk to Ava's boyfriend, Oliver."

"Sounds good," I said. "I'm looking forward to getting some sleep." The phone my father had given me also seemed to burn in my pocket. Once Trevor had left, I'd place a call to Jacob.

After locking the door behind him, I watched out the front window until he'd pulled out onto the street and rounded the corner. Only then did I fish the phone out.

There was one number programmed in the contacts. I dialed it and Vic answered.

"Everything okay?" he asked.

"Yes. I just met Brandy."

"I met her as well. Kind of a trip, huh?"

"Yes." I sighed and turned off the lights, then sat down next to Daisy in the dark. "I can't think about her right now, though. I'd like to talk to Jacob."

"Hang on."

I waited a long moment, then my son came on the phone. "Hey, Mom."

Tears welled in my eyes as I smiled. "Are you okay?"

"I'm good. My headache's gone."

"Great. I'm so happy to hear that. I'm going to find out who did this, Jacob."

"I know you will."

My son was safe. Nothing else mattered. If I was going to be effective in finding the killer, I needed some sleep. "I'll call you tomorrow and let you know where we are with the investigation, okay?"

"Sounds good."

"In the meantime, you lay low, Jacob. If Mallory catches you, there's nothing I can do to help you."

"I will, Mom. Right now, Vic and I are eating chili. He's stinking up the place, so I wish he would've skipped the beans, but everything is good. I promise, she'll never find me."

I prayed he was right.

CHAPTER 10

Mustard and Daisy made sure I was up early.

"Gina! Gina!" Daisy yelled. "Mustard has to pee!"

Even though the sun hadn't quite made an appearance, I was very happy I got her outside before she made a mess in the house. I took that as a sign it would be a good day.

After three cups of coffee and checking my email, I took the dogs for a walk. Mustard had some work to do on her leash skills, but I expected that. I watched her carefully so I didn't get the leash wrapped around my feet and fall to the ground. She did get tied up around Daisy's paws a few times, and I admired my dog's patience with the little one. I worried it wouldn't last long, though. Mustard was all over Daisy, nipping at her nose and barking at her while trying to play.

Finally, Daisy growled and rested her paw on Mustard's head until the puppy calmed down and we continued on our way.

In order to find Mustard a forever home, she needed a clean bill of health. She seemed quite robust, even though she'd been left in a dumpster. An appointment with the vet would be needed—I should've done it before bringing her into the house, which would have been standard protocol under normal circumstances. Funny how my son being accused of murder had rearranged my priorities.

It would be best if I could leave the two dogs home while Trevor and I interviewed Oliver, but first I had to make sure Daisy was up for the job and hadn't slipped into retirement, as she'd proclaimed the night before.

While she and Mustard sniffed a spot on our neighbors' lawn, I pulled out my phone and hoped I hadn't missed a call from Trevor.

Nothing. It wasn't even eight yet, so perhaps my impatience was getting the best of me.

"Daisy, can you watch Mustard again today?" I asked. I waited for an answer, but none came. "Daisy?"

"Hang on, Gina. I'm teaching Mustard the difference between dog pee and bunny pee. This spot has both."

Important stuff in the dog world.

Finally, when the lesson was over, Daisy said, "Yes, I can watch her. Don't be gone too long, okay?"

"I won't. We're going to talk to a guy Ava was seeing named Oliver. I'll be home after that."

"Okay. That sounds fair."

When we finished up the walk and arrived at our house, we found Trevor sitting on the porch swing, his head tilted up to the sun.

"Trevor! Trevor!" Daisy yelled as she pulled on the leash. "Trevor! Hi, Trevor!"

I let her go while Mustard barked, trying to follow her mentor. Daisy wouldn't dare run away, but I had no way of knowing about Mustard since I couldn't communicate with her. I kept her on the leash and hurried up to the porch where Trevor was smiling and petting Daisy. Mustard whined and barked, attempting to move in between them while Daisy kept pushing her out of the way.

"Gina, tell her that she has to wait her turn," Daisy said. "I've known Trevor the longest, so I should get petted first."

I grinned and sat down next to him. "Your uniform is going to be covered in dog hair."

"That's the least of my worries," he muttered, then scooped up Mustard and rubbed her chin while her little tail slapped against his ribcage. "I can't get over how cute this one is."

"What happened that's given you so many worries?" I asked.

"Gina! Don't let him pet Mustard!" Daisy yelled.

"Well, Mallory is in a tizzy—"

"Gina!"

"Let's go inside," I interrupted. Taking Mustard from him I set her down next to Daisy. "I'll make some coffee and you can tell me about Mallory's tizzy."

Once we were in the foyer, I unhooked the leashes from the dogs and they took off for the kitchen.

"Gina!" Daisy called. "We're hungry!"

"Let me get them fed," I said. "Take a seat in the living room and I'll get you some coffee." Sometimes I was glad Trevor couldn't hear my conversations with Daisy or he'd realize just how much she ruled around my house.

A few moments later, I handed him a mug and sat down next to him. "Good morning, by the way." I planted a quick kiss on his cheek. "So, what's Mallory's deal?"

He took a long sip, then sighed and met my gaze. "She wants me to arrest you for aiding and abetting a fugitive."

A moment of panic gripped me, but I quickly relaxed. My brother had done me a huge favor by keeping me in the dark on where he was taking Jacob. "I don't know where he is, though."

"I know. I believe you. I'm just telling you what's got her hackles up this morning."

A small part of me was quite pleased, and I tried to hide my smile by sipping my coffee.

Trevor narrowed his gaze. "I've known you long enough to realize you're very happy with yourself."

"Yes, I am. Anytime I can get under that woman's skin, I'm thrilled."

"She probably feels the same about you."

I shrugged and nodded. "Probably. Let me know if I need to call Colin Breckshire for my own defense."

"Will do. I don't think we're there yet. I told her I'd come speak to you about Jacob's whereabouts, but she knows we're seeing each other. I wouldn't be a bit surprised if she sent someone else out here to question you."

"I'll be ready because I truly don't have any information."

"And I can't be seen dragging you to question suspects."

"Are you leaving me here?" I asked. I hoped not.

"I know we said we were going to talk to Oliver today, but it's not going to happen with him living in town. We can go speak with Gabriel, though, because he lives out of town aways. No one will see us there. But the other kids... I may have to have you stay behind."

As I sipped my java, I considered his statement. There was no way I was going to be sidelined in speaking to the suspects. I had to find the killer to save Jacob. I'd speak to everyone involved, with or without him.

We sat in silence for a long moment and finished our coffee. "Ready to head out?" he asked.

"Let me just say goodbye to the dogs." I stood and grabbed the coffee cups and returned them to the kitchen. Based on the sounds coming from the bedroom, I'd find the dogs there. I hurried down the hall to discover Daisy on top of the bed teasing Mustard, who couldn't quite make the jump.

"Come on, Musty! Jump! Make those little sausage legs work!"

"Daisy, I'm leaving now," I whispered. Bending over, I scooped up the puppy and placed her on the comforter. "Are you two going to be okay?"

"Sure, we will!" Daisy yelled, her tail wagging in a blur. "We're going to play and play!" She nudged Mustard with her nose, sending her yelping to the carpet, then she laughed hysterically. "Did you see that, Gina? She rolls like a bowling ball!"

"Please be nice." I picked up Mustard again and set her down on the bed, deciding to play Daisy at her own game. "She could get hurt," I said. "And *good dogs* don't hurt their friends."

Daisy's tail came to a halt. "I see what you did there."

Smiling, I leaned over and kissed her nose. "Be a good dog. Don't toss Mustard off the bed anymore."

My lifeline to Jacob—the phone—laid on my nightstand. I considered leaving it, but if Mallory raided my house while I was gone, she'd find it. I grabbed it, made sure it was off, then headed out.

"We're good dogs," Daisy called as I walked

down the hall. "We'll be so good, you won't believe it!"

"Did Daisy tell you everything would be okay while you're gone?" Trevor asked, smirking.

He thought he was being cute and funny, but little did he know. "Aren't you adorable. Yes, she did. Let's go."

Our twenty-minute drive to Gabriel's house was long by Heywood standards. Usually, I could go where I needed to go in under ten. I sat back and enjoyed the thick forest sandwiching the road. So many trees, so much wildlife living among them.

We pulled off the highway and ended up in a nice, middle-class community. The cookie-cutter tidy houses indicated people took pride in their property. When we found the correct address, Trevor sighed.

"What's wrong?" I asked as I studied the white house with dark brown trim. The huge Palo Verde in front was in bloom with what seemed like a million little yellow flowers weighing down its branches and covering the ground beneath it. Personally, I hated the tree because of my allergies.

"I feel bad for this kid," Trevor replied. "He

found the bodies. When I talked to him yesterday morning at the crime scene, he was pretty distraught. He had thought everyone there was dead."

"That would be scary," I said.

"He was really shaken up and almost incoherent. I hope he's feeling better today and is willing to talk."

I exited the car and immediately began sneezing. Silently, I cursed the tree as we walked up to the front door. It opened before we got the chance to knock.

A middle-aged woman answered. Short and round, she wore her black hair up in a bun. She was dressed in jeans and a red t-shirt, with a yellow dishrag thrown over her shoulder. "Can I help you?" she asked in a thick Mexican accent.

"Mrs. Alverez?" Trevor pulled out his badge. "I was wondering if I could have a word with Gabriel."

"He's not feeling well," she said. "Yesterday was very hard for him." She pulled the dishrag from her shoulder and began squeezing it and threading it through her fingers, as if she was nervous. "Is he in trouble?"

"No," Trevor replied. "But I do have a dead

woman and I'd really like to find her killer. He was there, and I'm hoping he can give me more information today than he could yesterday."

"He loved Ava," she said quietly. "He'd never hurt that girl, even though she broke up with him."

"What about his friends he attended her party with?" I asked. Maybe if Gabriel hadn't killed her, one of his friends had. "Does he run with a good crowd?"

She shrugged. "You never know anymore. They come around and say all the right things, but kids are kids, especially at that age. They're dumb and full of themselves."

I wouldn't consider Jacob either of those things, but I was biased. What I did know was that he was innocent and I needed to find his killer.

"Can we talk to Gabriel?" I asked.

"Come on in." She sighed and shook her head. "Let me see if I can get him up."

We entered the foyer and I noted all the family photos in red frames placed with care up on the yellow walls. The bright color contrast was lively and unique.

"Does Gabriel go to the college?" I asked. A picture of him in a cap and gown surrounded by his family caught my eye. I assumed it was high school graduation. No one had confirmed that Gabriel went to school with the rest of the kids at the party, so I wanted to be sure to do so.

"Yes, he does," she said. She smiled with delight. "He's the first one in our family to get a college education and he's doing it on a full ride scholarship. We are so proud."

"That's wonderful," I said, sincerely. "Congratulations."

"Thank you. Let me go get him."

As we waited, I studied the pictures further. One with Gabriel and who I assumed to be his father with a boat caught my eye. Gabriel held a rope attached to the boat and his father had his arm around him. Proof Gabriel knew boats... and ropes. I nudged Trevor and pointed at it. He studied it, raised an eyebrow and nodded.

A soft breeze came through the screen door. I did love spring in Arizona. Up in the mountains, we had a true season of renewal with cool mornings and warm afternoons. Soon, it would warm up to the heat of summer and our area would be bustling with tourists. I didn't appreciate the congestion, but it was a huge boost to the Heywood economy.

The rustling of the yellow flowers across the rocks caught my attention and I turned just in time to see a young man sprinting across the front yard.

I elbowed Trevor, then rushed for the door. "He's running!"

CHAPTER 11

TREVOR CURSED behind me as we dashed across the yard through all those darn little flowers. My allergies went crazy, and I began sneezing, over and over again, my pursuit coming to a halt. Trevor hurried past me, leaving me in a flurry of evil flowers and pollen.

My eyes began to swell as I stumbled toward where Trevor had tackled Gabriel and was straddled on his back.

"Why are you running?" Trevor yelled. "Where you going, bud?"

"Don't cuff me!" Gabriel yelled. "Please! I didn't do anything!"

As Trevor breathed heavily while patting him down, Gabriel's mother came running out of the house. She broke out into a flurry of

Spanish. When she knelt down next to him and wagged her finger in his face, I didn't need a translator to understand she was mad at her son. "If you don't have anything to hide, then you don't run, *chico estupido*!"

I did understand *stupid* when I heard the word in just about any language.

The mother and son had a quick conversation in Spanish, then she stood to her full height. "I'm sorry, officers. He won't run again. He's scared."

Trevor slowly stood. "What's he scared of?"

"He's afraid he's going to prison for a crime he didn't commit."

"We'll make sure if he goes to prison, he deserves to be there," Trevor said. He yanked on Gabriel's arm and pulled him to his feet. "I'm not looking to railroad an innocent man. Now, can we have a conversation?"

"Yes." His mother shot her son a look that could've melted metal. "He'll tell you everything he knows."

We all returned to the house and filed into the kitchen. I ran a hand over my head and a couple of flowers fell to the table as I sat down. Silently, I cursed those stupid trees.

"Would you like a tissue?" Mrs. Alverez asked.

"That would be wonderful," I replied. "Thank you."

"I think your eyes are swelling," she said.

"It's the Palo Verde tree," I mumbled. "I'm allergic."

"Yes, you most certainly are." She stood and fetched a box of tissues, setting it down in front of me.

As I blew my nose, Trevor glared at Gabriel, then said, "Okay, buddy. Let's talk."

"I already told you everything I know when I spoke to you at the crime scene."

"Tell it all to me again," Trevor said. "All of it."

"I went to the party and then I left. I came back and found everyone. I saw the rope around Ava's neck and that guy holding it who had killed her... I called the police."

That guy being my son. My hands clenched in my lap hearing his interpretation of what happened, and I bit my tongue to keep from setting him straight: *My son hadn't killed anyone.*

"Were you invited to the party?" I asked, recalling that Bianca had indicated he hadn't been welcome.

He shook his head. "Ava had broken up with me. I was out with some friends and I heard through the grapevine that she was having a party. I decided to go and try to talk some sense into her."

"What sense is that?" I asked.

"That we were good together, that we belonged with each other. That her boyfriend was a jerk."

"Why do you think Oliver was a jerk?" I asked. "Did you hear something about the way he treated her, or did you think that because she chose him over you?"

Gabriel stared at me steadily as if weighing my words. "He was cheating on her."

"And she was cheating on him with you." I shrugged. "Does that make both of them jerks?"

"I... I don't know," he mumbled.

Let him sit with that for a bit.

After a moment, I continued. "I was also told that you left a couple of threatening voicemails for Ava after she broke up with you. Something about her regretting her decision?"

He muttered something in Spanish and shook his head. "I was hurt and said some things I probably shouldn't have."

"Did you threaten her?" I pushed. Out of the corner of my eye, I noted Trevor jotting down some notes. He would be asking where I got this information that he apparently didn't have. It wasn't my fault Bianca spilled the tea to me, and not him.

"I don't remember," he said.

It came so fast, I barely saw it. The slap up the side of Gabriel's head from his mother sounded throughout the kitchen. "You're threatening girls who break up with you?" she hissed. "What is wrong with you?"

"I just said she'd be sorry, Mom! That's it! I didn't say I was going to kill her!"

They exchanged some more words in Spanish. When they were through, Mrs. Alvarez worked her jaw so hard, I wouldn't be surprised if she chased Gabriel around the house with a belt after we left. 'Angry' was an understatement.

"Did you have words with Ava's boyfriend, Oliver, while you were at the party?" I asked.

"Yeah."

"Can you tell us what was said?"

"Well, he told me to leave, that Ava didn't want me there. I said he looked like a dork in his costume. He was wearing some wide-legged pants and a shirt unbuttoned to his stomach. It was dumb."

"It was a 70s costume party," I said. Suddenly, I realized that I hadn't seen Jacob's costume at the hospital. Where had it gone? If any of the clothing belonged to Annabelle, she was going to have a hissy fit if it was missing.

"Yeah, Ava told me."

"So you did speak to her?" I urged.

He nodded. "Oliver said if I didn't leave, he was going to beat me senseless."

"You didn't flinch from his threat."

"No. I was ready to throw down. I hate that guy. Ava finally came outside and pushed Oliver inside. We talked for a few minutes."

"What did you two have to say to each other?"

"It was basically me begging her to take me back." He shrugged. "I was pretty pathetic."

"Where were your friends you came with?" Trevor asked.

"They'd gone back to the car by then," Gabriel replied. "They didn't want any trouble."

"Smart boys," Mrs. Alvarez mumbled. "Hopefully, they'll start to rub off on you."

Gabriel rolled his eyes.

"What exactly did you say to Ava?" I prodded.

"That I loved her and wanted to be with her."

"And her response?" Trevor asked.

"She said she was going to stay with Oliver, and then asked me to leave. She didn't want me fighting Oliver."

"And did you go?"

"After a while. I just... I felt like if I left, then it was truly over between us."

"So what did you do while you stuck around? Was Ava talking to you?"

He shook his head. "No. She went back inside. I had a beer and just kind of hung around. Finally, my friends came and got me, and we left."

"What time did you return?" Trevor asked.

"I already answered this."

"I know that. I'm verifying information. Answer it again."

"We cruised around for a bit, went to get something to eat—"

"Where?" I interrupted.

"At the fast-food burger place out on the highway. By then, it was early morning, late at night. The sun wasn't up yet, but I don't know what time it was. I dropped my friends off at their houses, then went back to Ava's."

"And that's when you found everyone," Trevor said.

Gabriel nodded. "At first, I thought they

were all dead." His eyes welled. "Scared me to death."

"Did you touch anyone?" I asked.

"Yes. Ava. I loosened the rope from her neck and felt for a pulse. I was going to pound the guy holding the rope, but then I realized I was in the middle of a murder scene, so I called the police.

Something was off, but I couldn't place my finger on it.

"Do you have any other questions?" Trevor asked me.

I shook my head as I eyed the young man. He met my stare, and his cold, hard gaze sent a chill down my spine. Was I sitting across the table from a killer?

"Do we need a lawyer?" Mrs. Alvarez asked.

Trevor shrugged. "That's up to you. If you think it's best that Gabriel has one, then yes."

"Why do I need a lawyer if I didn't do anything?" Gabriel asked.

"It's for your protection," Mrs. Alvarez stated. "I shouldn't have had you talk to these two today. I should've followed my gut."

I smiled, relieved she hadn't listened to that little voice. "We appreciate your time."

"We'll be in touch," Trevor said.

As I followed him out to the truck, I wondered why no one ever asked me to produce something identifying me as a police officer. Perhaps Trevor showing his was enough.

And I also considered Gabriel's account of the night Ava was murdered. "If he wanted Ava to himself, wouldn't he have killed Oliver instead?" I asked as Trevor opened the door for me.

He waited to answer until he was behind the wheel. "I don't know. Maybe he was thinking that if he couldn't have Ava, then no one would."

"What about Oliver?" I asked. "When are you interviewing him?"

"He's coming down to the station today. Unfortunately, you can't be there."

Not with Mallory there. But that didn't mean I couldn't speak to Oliver on my own.

"Where did you get the information about Gabriel threatening Ava?" Trevor asked.

"Bianca. I guess she trusted me a little more than she trusted you."

"I guess so," Trevor muttered. "We should just deputize you. People talk to you."

"Yeah, I practically do your job for you."

I smirked while he chuckled.

"I'm going to drop you off at home, Gina," he said. "Then I'll go interview Oliver and catch up with Mallory on the investigation. I'll stop by later today."

"Sounds good. Can't wait to hear what Oliver has to say."

He shook his head. "I don't know. I'm still betting on Terry as the killer. She fully admitted she drugged those kids to have time alone with Oliver. Getting rid of Ava with everyone passed out would be simple for her."

"You're right," I said. "But maybe Oliver became so enraged with Ava for cheating, he killed her. I don't think we can take him off the table as a suspect. Same goes for Gabriel. There's something not right with his story, but I can't figure out what it is."

"Of course they're all still suspects. Just telling you what my gut is telling me."

We rode the rest of the way in silence. After he pulled into the driveway, I was relieved to see that my porch was empty. No long-lost relatives had shown up unannounced.

Trevor leaned over and gave me a soft kiss. For a moment, all of my worries seemed to vanish.

"I'll talk to you later," he whispered. "I've got to get back to the station."

I exited the car and headed up to the front door. Before inserting my key, I glanced in the front window where I found Mustard and Daisy in a game of tug-of-war with a throw pillow from the couch.

Was this how she watched the puppy? By partaking in very bad dog behavior?

Both were oblivious to me watching them. I shook my head just as the pillow exploded and its white insides flew around the room.

With a sigh, I put my key in the door, then pushed it open and hurried inside.

Mustard stared up at me with her half of the pillow dangling from her mouth. Daisy froze for a second, then yelled, "What a bad puppy she is! Bad Mustard! I can't believe you'd do something like this!"

CHAPTER 12

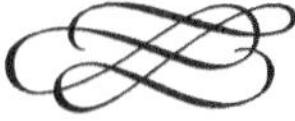

As I was about to scold my dog, my phone rang. I pulled it out of my pocket while glaring at Daisy.

"She did it!" Daisy shouted. She sat down and stared up at me with those big brown eyes that melted my heart. "I tried to stop her, Gina. I swear it! Puppies don't listen!"

Annabelle was calling.

"Hi," I answered, walking into the kitchen. "What's going on?"

"I heard about the mess at the Willard house," she said. "Some ladies were in Sage Advice gossiping. Like, what the heck, Gina?"

"Mess is an understatement." I sighed and sat down at the kitchen table and told her the whole horrid tale. "Sheriff Mallory thinks Jacob strangled Ava Willard."

"That may be the dumbest thing she's ever said."

"Well, there's evidence pointing to him. He had the end of the rope that strangled her in his hand."

She gasped. "Oh, my goodness! Where is he? Is he okay?"

"I don't know where he is, but he's fine."

"You don't know where your son is? But he's fine? How does that, like, work?"

"He's gone," I replied. "I don't know where he is, but I've been told he's fine. Leave it at that, okay?"

She muttered a curse under her breath. "I was calling to get the scoop and you aren't being helpful."

"I'm sorry, Annabelle. I honestly don't know where he is, and that's the way I want to keep it." It was time to change the conversation. "Jacob told me that you gave him the clothes for the party."

"I did. He looked so cute, didn't he?"

"Yes." I shut my eyes and placed my head in my hand, my elbow on the table. "I hate to tell you, but they're gone."

Silence filled the line for a long moment. "Where are they?"

"I'm guessing Mallory has them. They weren't at the hospital when I saw Jacob after the party."

"I hate her," Annabelle hissed. "Someone should strangle her. Those were vintage from eBay, straight out of the 70s."

She wouldn't hear an argument from me, but just in case my phone was tapped, I kept my mouth shut.

Speaking of which… I pulled out the other phone I had to call Jacob. I was both relieved and disappointed I hadn't missed any calls. At least I knew nothing had transpired requiring my attention.

"You're trying to find the killer, right?" Annabelle asked.

"Of course. I'm not letting Mallory railroad my son."

"Good. I have some information that you may find, like, helpful in your investigation."

"What's that?" I asked.

"Mrs. Willard is a client of mine." I heard the door chime on the other end, indicating someone had entered Sage Advice. "Hold on, Gina."

From then on, I heard muffled conversation. While she was helping her customer, I decided to have a chat with my dog.

I walked into the living room and began picking up the pillow stuffing. "Daisy, I saw you in the window," I said, propping the phone between my shoulder and ear. "I know you're just as responsible for this mess as Mustard is."

"I didn't do anything!" she whined.

"Daisy, *I saw you*," I repeated, rolling my eyes. "You once told me that good dogs don't lie. Remember?"

"I was trying to stop her from biting the pillow!" she yelled. "I wasn't playing!"

"Stop, Daisy. I saw you. Admit you were doing something you shouldn't have."

"Okay." She sat down and lowered her head. "You're right. I got carried away playing tug-of-war. I'm sorry."

With a sigh, I sat down next to her and set aside the remains of the pillow. I could still hear Annabelle talking to her customer, so I continued my conversation with my dog. "We weren't expecting Mustard, and frankly, she couldn't have shown up at a worse time. That's why I need you to help me, Daisy."

"I know." She leaned into me and placed her head on my lap. "I miss Jacob. Will he be home soon?"

"That's what I'm trying to accomplish," I said, stroking her chest.

"Taking care of a puppy is hard."

"Believe me, I'm aware." Speaking of which, where was Mustard? I turned to find her sitting in the corner by the couch. "Come here, Musty. I'm not mad. We all make mistakes."

She slowly approached and crawled into my lap, nose to nose with Daisy. As I waited for Annabelle to return, I petted my two charges. The stress I'd been feeling slowly began to fade. My shoulders relaxed and the knot in my stomach subsided.

"We promise to be better dogs, Gina," Daisy said. She licked Mustard's black button nose. "Isn't she cute? She's almost as cute as me."

"Almost."

"Someone is going to want her and that makes me sad."

It was the first time Daisy had been upset that a dog we rescued may be adopted and I wasn't sure what to say.

"Maybe we should keep her," Daisy continued.

I liked Mustard, but had no plans for a second dog. I preferred to use my resources to rescue the ones that were in dire straits and help them find forever homes.

Mustard barked at Daisy and bit her nose.

"Hey, you little twerp!" Daisy yelled. Both stood and Mustard bit Daisy's leg. "You better run, Mustard!"

As they took off down the hall, I stood and moved to the kitchen again. The two dogs raced by me into the living room, then back toward the bedroom, having a great time. Hopefully, they'd soon play themselves right into naptime.

"Sorry about that," Annabelle said. "What were we talking about?"

"I think you were going to tell me something about Mrs. Willard."

"Oh, that's right. Yes. Mrs. Willard is a client of mine. I mix a special tincture for her anxiety. That woman is wound tighter than a ball of yarn. When she's here, she tells me everything that is bothering her. Her husband is a big stressor, but so is Ava. Mrs. Willard worried about Ava going to college and she was afraid she'd make dumb choices and end up pregnant. She worried about money, even though to the outside eye, it doesn't look like they have any financial problems. It's like she searches for things to worry about, but she did say the tincture I make helps a lot."

I wasn't sure where this was going. "What does that have to do with Ava's murder?"

"Well, Mrs. Willard was in a few days ago to pick up the tincture. Of course, she started talking. She's always talking, like I'm her therapist or something. It can get a little annoying because she does overshare. She said that Ava had, like, picked up a stalker at school."

My blood ran cold. I stood and began pacing the kitchen. "A stalker? Did she give any details?"

"Yes. He was stalking her through social media and sending her inappropriate pictures via emails and texts."

"Are we sure it was a man?"

Annabelle sighed, then said, "Duh, Gina. When I say inappropriate pictures, what do you think I mean? Pictures of white, fluffy bunnies and flowers? I'm talking about up-close pictures of the one-eyed wonder weasel, if you know what I mean."

"Understood," I grumbled. "That was a dumb thing for me to ask."

"That's okay. You're allowed to be dumb every now and then."

"Did Mrs. Willard have any idea who it could be? Or what the stalker was saying to her daughter?"

"She didn't go into a lot of detail on that, but she's going to be here soon. She just got back into town and with Ava's murder, she's a mess. She's asked me to maximize the tonic so she can sleep."

As the dogs ran by the kitchen again, I debated whether I should head over to Sage Advice and blindside the poor mother or stay put in my house and wait for Trevor.

"I'd figure you'd want to be here," Annabelle continued. "I mean, Jacob has been accused of killing that poor girl and we, like, know he didn't."

She was right. I glanced into the living room at the pillow entrails still on the floor.

Most times when I went to see Annabelle at Sage Advice, I brought Daisy with me. But how would Mustard do in new surroundings? The last thing I needed was her peeing on the floor or finding something to chew on that she shouldn't. Annabelle was trying to run a business and she didn't need a puppy around.

However, I didn't think I could leave them by themselves in the house any longer.

"I'll be there shortly," I said. After hanging up, I shooed the dogs outside and told them to relieve themselves. Minutes later, we were on our way to Sage Advice.

"Yay!" Daisy yelled from the backseat. "I love Jack! Jack and I run and play and it's so much fun!"

"Make sure to include Mustard, okay?"

I glanced in back and found the little blonde fluffball sitting in the corner, seemingly unsure of this new escapade.

"Okay, Gina." Daisy leaned over and licked my cheek. "Mustard says she doesn't like car rides and she feels like throwing up."

"Oh, no," I groaned. "Is she going to be okay until we get there, or should I pull over?"

Daisy turned to the puppy while I watched them in the mirror. "She says she's going to be okay, but that bunny poop she ate earlier isn't sitting very well with her."

"You shouldn't have let her eat that."

"She did it so fast I didn't have time to tell her not to."

With a long sigh, I prayed Mustard was able to keep her stomach settled. Thankfully, we pulled in front of Sage Advice without any issues.

After I leashed the two dogs, Daisy led us toward the store while Mustard fought me by pulling and biting her tether. I didn't have the time or energy for a training session, so I scooped her up and we headed inside.

"Hi, Annabelle! Hi!" Daisy yelled. Her brown and white tail swished back and forth so fast, it was a blur. "Where's my friend, Jack? I want to play with Jack!"

"Oh, my gosh," Annabelle said as she approached wearing a Poison t-shirt and neon blue leggings that matched her eyeliner. "Who is that little monster of cuteness?"

"You know me!" Daisy replied. "I'm Daisy! Where's Jack?"

Fully aware that Annabelle was referring to the puppy in my arms and not my talking dog, I unhooked Daisy's leash and set her free. She ran through the store and into the back room. I assumed she'd be heading upstairs.

I was almost embarrassed to say the puppy's name. "Mustard," I replied.

Annabelle stared at her a long moment, then said, "Gina, that's, like, the most perfect name for her. Unique, yet cute, and totally fitting with her coloring."

Pursing my lips, I tried not to laugh at Annabelle being on the same wavelength as Daisy. I thought Mustard was a ridiculous name, but apparently, I knew nothing about naming a 'monster of cuteness.'

Mustard had quit squirming in my grasp and glanced around the store. Curious? Hesitant? I had no idea. I gently set her down, but she stayed next to me, so I leaned toward hesitant. She whined at my side as Jack and Daisy ran into the store and Jack stopped to give her a good once over with his nose.

"Come play with us, Mustard!" Daisy yelled, pushing the puppy with her nose. "We'll chase you!"

Mustard barked and Annabelle leaned over to pick her up. "She's just... she's just adorable. I can't believe how round she is."

"I was surprised by that too, especially since I found her in the dumpster."

"Poor thing," Annabelle said, holding her against her chest. Mustard glanced up and licked Annabelle's chin, then returned her attention back to Daisy and Jack wrestling at Annabelle's feet.

I heard the door open behind me. Glancing over my shoulder, I found a rail-thin woman about my age with long, scraggly blond hair hanging around her shoulders. Her red-rimmed sunken gaze met mine. She'd been crying. Sobbing. Heartbroken.

Without a doubt, it was Mrs. Willard.

I was about to introduce myself until I heard a retching sound. I turned around to find Mustard had vomited all over Annabelle.

CHAPTER 13

"Oh, my!" Annabelle exclaimed. She looked from me to Mrs. Willard, then back again. Both my friend and my puppy were covered in dog vomit. "Let me go get us cleaned up. I'll be right back, Mrs. Willard. It won't take long."

As Annabelle hurried through the store to her upstairs apartment, I turned back to Mrs. Willard and smiled, appreciating Mustard's timing and Annabelle's willingness to leave me with the grieving mother. "I'm sorry to hear about Ava."

She nodded, her face expressionless, almost as if she was drugged. "Me, too. At least they know who did it. When they find him, I hope he dies behind bars."

I glanced outside to see a man sitting in the

driver's seat of a car in front of the store. He stared out the windshield as if in deep thought. I assumed it to be Mr. Willard.

"I know that kid didn't have anything to do with it," I said. "I was hoping to hear about Ava's stalker, though."

She pushed her purse over her shoulder and wrung her hands as her gaze darted around the store. "Who are you?"

It was probably not in my best interest to reveal my name. If the roles were reversed, I wouldn't want to talk to the mother of the boy I was sure killed my daughter. "Someone who is trying to find the real killer."

"Are you some type of true crime investigator?"

"Something like that." Maybe I'd use that in the future if the need ever arose.

She nodded. "I've read about people like you. Even watched a couple of documentaries. Sometimes the police don't do a good job and regular people need to take over and get things done."

"I agree, and I think this is one of those times."

"But they found the boy with the rope in his hand!" she exclaimed. "How much more evidence do you need?"

"He was drugged," I said, keeping my voice even. "A few of them were. That rope could've been placed in his hand after the killer murdered Ava."

Tears welled in her eyes as she twisted her hands more frantically. I shouldn't have been so blunt with the mother of a dead girl.

"Listen," I said, gently laying my hand on her forearm. "I'm trying to find justice for your daughter—real justice. I don't want some kid being railroaded for something he didn't do."

As the tears streamed down her cheeks, I led her over to the counter and fetched a couple of stools from the back. "Let's sit down," I said. Once she was settled in, I pressed her for information. "Did your house have any cameras so that the police can review the footage?"

"No. I never wanted cameras on my property. I'd seen articles about people hacking into cameras and watching their victims. It scared me to death, but now I wish we'd had them."

I'd hoped they'd been hidden well and the police hadn't noticed them, but I pressed on as defeat rolled through me. "Can you tell me about the stalker?"

She sighed and shook her head. "Ava told me about him a couple of weeks ago. He was sending her lewd messages and leaving gross comments on her social media. I told her to go to the police."

"Is her social media still up?"

Mrs. Willard stared at me a long moment, then blinked twice. "I... I never thought to take it down."

"That's okay," I said quickly. The platforms could offer a great glimpse into Ava's life and reveal some clues. I was thrilled they were still active, but I made a mental note to study them as soon as I could. Hopefully Trevor had already done so, but I'd like to take a peek as well. "There are more important things to worry about now," I said. "Did Ava say she knew who the stalker was, Mrs. Willard?"

"No. And please, call me Gwen."

"Do you know if she went to the police?" I asked.

"She said she did," Gwen replied. "But she could've told me that to calm my worries."

"Is that something she did often? Lie to you?"

"Yes. I have terrible anxiety. She was concerned about me, and I've found out over the years that she lied in order to help me."

A child shouldn't feel responsible for their mother's anxiety. It was a heavy weight to carry, and in my opinion, quite unfair.

"Tell me about Ava," I urged. "She obviously cared deeply for you. What was she like?"

She pulled a tissue from her purse and dabbed her eyes. "She was... she was so different from me. She was alive. There was no fear, and there never had been. When she was little, her father referred to her as his sweet, little hurricane. There was always so much energy there, sometimes she frightened me."

"What scared you?"

"Her lack of fear, I suppose." She shrugged. "I've always been a worrier and to give birth to a child who was afraid of nothing... it was quite the lesson for me, quite the shock."

"Can you give me an example?"

"When she was little, she used to jump off the back of the couch and tell me she was learning to fly. One day, I caught her playing with a snake outside. In high school, she wanted to go to a dance with a specific boy. Instead of waiting for him to ask her, she asked him. Things I would never do. I think we expect our children to be some sort of mirror of us before they're born. I did, anyway. And Ava wasn't."

I certainly wouldn't refer to Jacob as my mirror image, but we did have a lot of the same personality traits. Thankfully, he had seemed to have bypassed most of my bad ones.

"That's understandable," I said. "How did Ava do at school?"

"She always wanted to be the best at everything she did. Straight A's. Lots of friends. She joined every club she could and excelled at everything. I don't know where she got the energy."

"Did she have any guesses on where she could've picked up this stalker? Maybe a party? Or someone at school she had angered?"

"I don't know," Gwen replied. "She was quite competitive. Throughout high school, she sometimes alienated people with her fierce desire to win at all costs. That went for sports and clubs."

I recalled Jacob sharing the conflict between Zoe and Ava at the party. "It was my understanding that there was more than a little healthy competition between Ava and a girl on the debate team named Zoe. Did she share any details with you?"

"She disliked Zoe with a passion."

"Why?"

After tucking a lock of hair behind her ear, Gwen glanced around the store as if searching for the correct words. "Honestly, I think it was because Zoe made Ava work for every win. I witnessed them at a debate and Zoe was incredibly smart and a fast thinker. Ava hated it when someone was better than her, and Zoe was."

"How much did Ava dislike her?"

"Privately, she had some choice words about Zoe. If Ava had a fault, it was that she wasn't a graceful loser. She'd smile and seem to take the loss with dignity, but when she was out of the public eye, she'd throw a tantrum."

"Did you know Ava was having a party that night?" I asked.

Mrs. Willard shook her head. "And I'm shocked she invited Zoe."

Why go to a party she wasn't wanted at? Gabriel showing up, I understood. He was trying to win back his girlfriend. But Zoe? Maybe she didn't have a clue how deeply Ava disliked her, even though Jacob had said it was evident.

"Do you know her boyfriend, Oliver?"

"We've met him quite a few times. He seems like a nice guy, but I didn't get the feeling he was the one, you know?"

"Why was that?"

"He was... boring isn't the right word. Oliver was always perfectly charming and polite. He just wasn't a match for Ava's energy."

I had to tread carefully with my next questions. I didn't want to soil her daughter's memory, but I had to ask about Ava's side piece.

"Did Ava ever mention a guy named Gabriel?"

"No. Was she dating him on the side?"

When I didn't answer, she gave me a sad smile. "I figured as much. Like I said, Oliver was far too passive for Ava. She needed more. Tell me about Gabriel."

"He's a student at the college," I said. "Seems like a nice kid."

"Is he smart?"

"Yes. He's on a full ride scholarship. Ava had recently broken up with him."

She arched an eyebrow. "Do you think that maybe he's her stalker? Ava mentioned the lewd notes and things to me a couple of weeks ago. When did they break up?"

"I don't have exact dates, but from what I understand, they were on and off for a while."

"So it's possible."

"I suppose so."

"Oh, my."

"Is there anyone else you know who would want to hurt Ava?" I asked.

"Not that I can think of. Did Oliver know about Gabriel?"

"I believe so. Do you think he could've killed her?"

Slowly shaking her head, she said, "I just don't know anything anymore. Ava's death has left me questioning everyone and everything. My brain is a muddled mess."

We sat in silence as I attempted to think of more questions. Upstairs, Jack and Daisy ran back and forth and they sounded more like a couple of baby elephants, rather than two dogs.

"You said they were drugged." Gwen turned to me.

"Yes."

"Who did that? And why?"

I sighed and clasped my hands together in my lap. "There's a girl named Terry who had a crush on Oliver. She meant to drug Ava so she could have some time with Oliver without Ava knowing about it. Unfortunately, the kids started playing a game with the water bottle they all drank out of. Four of them were drugged."

"My goodness! What's wrong with her?!"

"I wondered the same thing. She seems to be somewhat troubled."

"That's an understatement. Do you think she could've killed Ava? Drugging her so she could make the moves on her boyfriend seems a little extreme. Why wouldn't she take it a step further?"

"I agree. She's definitely at the top of my list."

And I hoped someone was watching Oliver to see if she'd reached out to him. After I finished speaking with Gwen, I wanted to catch up with Trevor and hear about his interview with him.

Annabelle came bounding down the steps along with all the dogs. She smiled as she approached and I noted she'd swapped her Poison t-shirt for Def Leppard, and Mustard was wet.

"I had to give this little darling a bath," she said, handing her over to me.

"She's beautiful," Mrs. Willard said. "May I hold her?"

I passed Mustard to her. "Of course."

As she stroked the yellow fur, tears streamed down her face again. "What a sweetheart." Mustard settled against her and reached up to kiss her nose.

Had I found a home for Mustard? Daisy had shared that it wasn't the humans who picked the dogs, but the dogs who picked the humans. Mustard seemed quite comfortable in Mrs. Willards arms.

"I have your tincture ready to go whenever

you are," Annabelle said. "I wish there was something to do to take away your pain."

"So do I," Gwen replied, now sobbing as she cradled Mustard. "So do I."

My resolve to find the killer only deepened, if that was possible. I'd been so focused on clearing Jacob's name, I hadn't given any thought to Ava's family. Would Gwen ever recover from her daughter's death? Would she be able to smile and experience joy again?

I had no idea, but if I were in her shoes, knowing that the murderer who had taken something so precious from me was behind bars would be the first step in getting my life back.

A horn blared outside and I turned to find the man in the car glaring at the store. "Is that your husband?" I asked.

She nodded and handed Mustard back to me. "He's a bit impatient. Will you keep me updated on your investigation? I'm not sure who to trust anymore."

"Of course I will," I said. "Let's trade numbers. I'm going to nail whoever did this to your daughter, Gwen. I promise."

CHAPTER 14

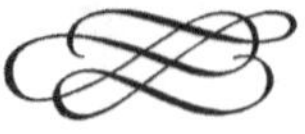

THANKFULLY, Mustard had kept what was left of her stomach contents to herself on the way home. When we arrived, I sent the dogs outside. Then I pulled out the phone I used to contact Jacob. He answered on the second ring.

"Hi, honey. Is it safe to talk?"

"Yeah. I'm watching reruns of *Friends*. Why didn't you tell me about this show? I think Ross is right. They were on a break."

I laughed. "I've only recently started re-watching it myself," I said. "I'd forgotten how fun it is. And while you were growing up, I was too busy to watch it."

"But you spent hours watching *Backyardigans* with me."

"And that was much more fun than

Friends. Listen, I was wondering if you've remembered anything else about the party."

"Not really. I feel like there are memories I can't quite get to, like they're just out of reach."

With a sigh, I closed my eyes. I hoped some recollections came back soon. Or maybe, they wouldn't at all, especially with the drugs. I needed more clues from him on what happened that night.

"Okay, keep me posted," I said. "Do you know what Zoe's parents do or where I can locate her last name?"

"Hmm... oh, I know! Check the school website and look for the debate team. I bet it's listed there."

I smiled, impressed with my son. "What a great idea, Jacob. Thanks. I'll take a look. Hang on."

After fetching my laptop from the bedroom, I hurried back into the kitchen and sat down at the table while holding the phone between my shoulder and cheek. In a few minutes, I'd found the debate team listing. "Zoe Brusher." I scribbled it down on a piece of paper. "Is she a local? I don't recognize the name."

"She told me at the party she lives in

Flagstaff."

Brown, curly hair fell to her shoulders, framing her pretty olive-skinned face and bright smile. "She's beautiful," I said.

"That's why Eric wanted to stay at the party," he replied. "If Zoe hadn't been there, we would've left and I wouldn't be in this position. It was love at first sight for him."

"You can't blame him for falling for a pretty girl," I said.

"Well, I kind of do, Mom."

"Life is a series of choices," I replied. "Sometimes they seem innocuous, like they don't matter. But each decision that's made leads us down a different path. Eric chose to stay at the party to hopefully get to know Zoe better, and you stayed with him because he's been your friend for years."

"And now the sheriff thinks I killed Ava."

Unfortunately for Mallory, she'd made a very bad decision pursuing my son. I'd make sure she paid. "And we're going to prove her wrong."

We sat in silence for a long moment while I studied Zoe's picture. "Why was she at the party if she and Ava didn't get along?" I mused.

"She said she was invited."

"But why would Ava invite someone she didn't like?"

Jacob sighed. "I have no idea, Mom. Maybe she was trying to impress her or something?"

"Impress her how?"

"I don't know. I'm just throwing stuff against the wall and seeing what sticks. I personally wouldn't invite someone I didn't like to my party, but Zoe was adamant that Ava had."

"Did you know Ava had a stalker?"

Jacob gasped. "No, kidding. Wow. I had no idea."

I skipped over to Instagram and looked her up. Like most young people, Ava lived her life on social media. A lot of selfies populated her page, along with pictures of her and her friends.

"Brandy's coming over today," Jacob said.

For a second, I had no idea who he was talking about, then I recalled that was my mothers' name. Frankly, I was envious she got to see my son and I didn't, but I tried to keep it out of my voice. "Oh, really?"

"Yes. I tried to call her Grandma and she said not to. She wants me to call her Brandy."

For some reason, that brought me some satisfaction. She hadn't earned the title and she realized it.

"Are you seeing a lot of her?"

"She's stopped by a couple of times."

"Do... do you like her?" I almost hoped he didn't. At least that way I could cut her out of my life and tell myself it was for Jacob's benefit.

"Yeah, I do. She reminds me a lot of you."

I wanted to ask in what way, but decided finding a killer was more important. I'd always been best at ignoring things and, in this case, people I didn't want to deal with. "That's great, honey. I'm going to get back to work and I'll speak to you soon."

"Okay. Love you, Mom. Thanks for everything."

"Love you, too."

I set my phone down and returned to Ava's social media. It didn't take long to find the comments from the stalker.

You look like a pig in this picture. Oink, oink you ugly troll.

Good thing you're so smart because your butt is so big, I could write Massachusetts across it and have room left over for Rhode Island.

· · ·

HOW DO you look at your ugly face every morning knowing what a horrible person you are?

GO DIE SOMEWHERE ALONE.

AND THEN THE PROFANITY. Such colorful language, some of it even impressed me. "I've never thought to use that word as a verb," I mumbled.

Why would she keep them up for all to see?

The author's name was 4Zr54Og9yt9E. Obviously, someone who didn't want their name revealed. Maybe a throwaway account.

I couldn't for the life of me figure out why she'd keep these comments up, so I kept reading and soon had an answer.

OH, my gosh! You aren't ugly, queen! Who would say that about you?

I WOULD KILL to have a butt like yours! Don't listen to the haters, girl!

· · ·

THAT TROLL only wishes she or he could be as smart and cute as you.

THEN AVA COMMENTED, thanking everyone for the support. It seemed she liked the responses, which fell in line with what everyone had told me about her. She appreciated being the center of everything, being the best. These hateful comments fueled her friends to stick up for her and drew attention to her.

But was it a man? I recalled Annabelle saying Ava had received nasty pictures. I could only see what was public. I assumed Trevor had her phone and was diving into her texts.

I stared at the hater's name. Something about it intrigued me, but I couldn't place my finger on what it was.

Whoever the stalker was, they despised Ava and let her know. Had they'd been at the party? Did they dislike her enough to kill her, or just to hassle her online? This seemed like the best suspect and I had to assume the stalker was the same person who had murdered her. The fact they'd told her to go die seemed like a credible threat to me.

If Ava's picture was on the school website for the debate team, then maybe I could find Oliver. Had anyone told me if he was in any clubs?

I scrolled through the rest of the debate team and didn't find anyone named Oliver. I had no idea about his last name, but how many kids these days were called Oliver?

Next, I went to the other clubs. Just as I was about to give up, I saw his name. He wrote for the newspaper and also was a member of the poetry club.

Brown hair with green eyes and a soft smile, he was handsome and gave off vibes of safety. Definitely not a bad boy full of himself with too much testosterone running through him.

Yet, he seemed to be somewhat of a ladies man if Terry was willing to drug his girlfriend so she could have a shot with him. Bianca had also indicated she thought Oliver was cheating on Ava. Had that been with Terry? Perhaps Terry and Oliver worked together that night to get Ava out of the way. If she'd been drugged, then there wouldn't have been any fight while someone killed her. She'd simply gone to sleep and never woken up while being strangled.

"I think I like this idea," I said to the empty kitchen. I just needed to clear Zoe so I could focus on my theory. And that meant driving to Flagstaff. A quick internet search garnered me her parent's address. I imagined she lived at home since her house was so close to the school.

"Gina! Gina!" Daisy shouted. "Let us in!"

I'd been so consumed with the murder, I'd completely forgotten about the dogs outside. After letting them in, I made a quick decision. I wanted to talk to Zoe, but I couldn't leave the dogs at home. Still, it wouldn't be fair to Mustard or me if I took her and she became sick in the car.

But what to do with them? I wasn't going to risk another pillow incident. I needed a dog sitter, so I called Annabelle.

"What's going on, Gina?" she answered.

"Can you watch Mustard and Daisy for a bit?"

"Of course. Bring them back to the store."

"No!" Daisy whined. "Gina, I want to be with you! Please take me wherever you're going!"

"I'm sorry, Annabelle," I amended. "It will just be Mustard. Is that okay?"

"Yay!" Daisy yelled. "I get to be with my human! Yay!"

"Of course. Come on by. Where are you off to?"

"Flagstaff," I said as I picked up Mustard and motioned Daisy toward the door. "There was a girl at the party named Zoe. I'm going to talk to her."

"Okay. Keep me posted on what you find out."

I hurried back to Sage Advice, dropped off Mustard, then Daisy and I set out for Flagstaff.

"I probably should call Trevor," I muttered.

"Forget Trevor!" Daisy shouted, then licked the side of my face. "It's Daisy and Gina for once! With your brains and my super sniffer, we can do anything!"

I laughed, then changed the subject. "How are things going with Mustard? What type of family do you think should adopt her?"

"We should adopt her, Gina. She's my goofy little buddy."

"She's not going to be little for long. I think she's got some Golden Retriever in her. Maybe a bit of lab."

"So, she's going to be bigger than me and

maybe a very bad dog. Then she'll be my big buddy and boss me around."

"Exactly."

"Well, I don't think I like that," Daisy replied. "I want to be the boss."

"You pretty much are now."

"I know. I want to keep it that way and I don't like bad dogs. I have to think about Mustard. Maybe after my nap. She makes me tired."

She curled up in the backseat and shut her eyes.

Meanwhile, I drove the rest of the way in silence, my mind churning with what I would discover after speaking to Zoe. Maybe I should've phoned Trevor and gotten some contact information on her. But then he'd forbid me from seeing her alone, and demand I wait for him. Patience wasn't one of my stronger attributes.

The GPS on my phone took me to the address. Located in a well-kept neighborhood, I admired the daffodils and petunias coming up in front of the yellow and white house. My heart sank when I noted there wasn't a vehicle in the driveway but there was a boat. Like Gabriel, it seemed that Zoe had spent some time around them, which meant she'd also worked with the ropes.

"Wait until I tell Trevor about this," I muttered.

"Stay here," I said to Daisy as I removed my seatbelt. I hoped all residents parked in the garage and someone would be home. Driving all this way for nothing would be quite disappointing. "I won't be very long."

"Okay, Gina."

I hurried up to the front door and rang the doorbell. No answer. I knocked and considered going around into the backyard, but then I noticed the camera pointed at me from the corner of the porch.

These days, everyone had cameras. Everyone except the Willards. If they'd had their house wired up, this whole mess would've been over by now.

So, no sneaking around for me.

I returned to my car and shut the door, unsure what my next steps should be. Perhaps returning to Heywood and waiting for Trevor to call was the smartest.

"Gina, look at those people down the street," Daisy said. "They're licking face!" She slurped her tongue up my cheek.

I hadn't noticed the park at the end of the block, nor the two people sitting on the bench underneath the blossoming cherry tree kissing, or licking face, as Daisy had so eloquently put it.

After pushing my glasses up my nose, I squinted and was able to make out curly brown hair on one of the people.

"Is that... is that Zoe?" I asked. "And who is she kissing?"

CHAPTER 15

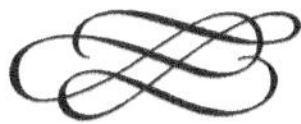

"I DON'T KNOW who Zoe is," Daisy said. "Should I know Zoe? Is she a friend of ours?"

"No, we don't know her personally," I said, then made a hasty decision. "We're going for a walk."

"Yay! I love walks!"

I glanced around the car. "Where's your leash?"

"You didn't bring it. Good dogs don't need a leash, and despite the pillow incident, I am a very good dog."

I sighed and turned my attention back to the two at the end of the block. I was pretty sure that was Zoe, but they hadn't come up for breath, so I couldn't be certain. "I need you to stay right next to me, Daisy. Do you understand?"

"Yes."

"Can you do that?"

"Probably."

It was better than no. As I scanned the street, I didn't see any cats or other dogs to chase. I just wanted to get closer to the couple and what was a better way to do that than to walk my dog in the park?

"We're going to play this cool," I said. "We're just out for a stroll. They won't even notice us."

"I'm sure you're right."

"Okay, let's do this." I exited the car and opened the back door to let Daisy out. She stood right at my side. "Good girl."

"Thank you. I told you I'm a good dog."

As we strolled up the sidewalk, I kept my gaze firmly on the couple. The beautiful park was surrounded by tall pines full of singing birds. To the left stood a children's play structure. About an acre of grass stretched before us. Benches had been strategically placed so all could enjoy natures' wonderment. Daisy and I sat on the bench not far from the lovebirds.

"If he smashes his face into hers anymore, it's going to break her nose," Daisy said.

Yes, they were really getting into it.

"Oh, my gosh, Gina." Daisy stood with her tail straight out behind her and stared into the trees on the other side of the park. As her ears perked, she said, "Look at that."

I turned to where she was referring and saw nothing. "What is it?" I whispered.

"A squirrel," she said. "That little rodent is taunting me."

"I don't think so," I replied. "It's probably just going on about its little squirrel life."

"Oh, no. He's making fun of me, telling me that I can't catch him."

"Daisy, he's not. You don't speak squirrel."

"I don't need to speak squirrel to know his thoughts. He's begging me to chase him."

"You promised me you'd stay right by my side."

"I know."

"You said you were a good dog."

"I am. But what about my pride? This squirrel is teasing me, Gina. Challenging me to catch him."

"Daisy, he is not. This is all in your imagination." And maybe this dumb conversation was in mine. "Stay where you are."

A low growl escaped her throat as the muscles in her haunches quivered.

"Don't even think about it," I hissed.

As I reached over to grab her collar, she bolted away from me, barking incessantly while running toward the trees.

"Daisy!" I yelled.

The noise was enough to break up Zoe and her friend. To my utter shock, I had been right in recognizing Zoe's hair, but I never would've guessed she was kissing Oliver, Ava's boyfriend, of all people. I recalled Bianca telling me she thought Oliver was cheating on Ava, but I never imagined it would be with Zoe.

My disbelief was so great, I forgot about Daisy trying to climb a tree and marched over to the couple while different scenarios crossed my mind. Zoe got rid of Ava so she could be with Oliver, or visa versa. Maybe they'd planned it together and *set up my son to take the fall!*

"Isn't this cozy," I spat, my fury rising with each passing moment. Standing in front of them, I crossed my arms over my chest. "Oliver, for the boyfriend who is supposed to be mourning the loss of his beloved girlfriend, Ava, you sure have moved on quickly."

He stared at me with wide eyes, his mouth hanging open. I also remembered he was supposed to be in Heywood speaking with Trevor, who would be absolutely furious when he found out Oliver had skipped their meeting to be with his secret love.

"And you, Zoe. Competition between you and Ava was fierce, but here you are slobbering all over her boyfriend. That's low, girl. As low as you can go."

I was glad Jacob's friend, Eric, didn't stand a chance with the girl. She was too wrapped up in Oliver, and Eric deserved better than her.

"Wait a minute," Oliver said, standing. "Who are you?"

My idea in coming to Flagstaff had been to speak to Zoe in a civilized way. This confrontation wasn't in my plan, but I'd roll with it. I wouldn't reveal my true identity, though.

"I'm the person who's going to find out who killed Ava. So spill it. Getting her out of the picture was a benefit for both of you, wasn't it?"

Oliver sat down and they exchanged glances. Finally, he said, "Ava and I were basically over. I don't know why neither of us ended it."

"How long have you two been an item?" I asked, pointing at them.

"A few months," Zoe replied.

"Why don't you both tell me what happened the night Ava was killed? Zoe, why were you there at the party?"

"I was invited." She shrugged. "At first, I didn't understand why, but Ava said she wanted me there, to put our rivalry behind us."

"But you two argued instead," I urged.

Zoe nodded. "We did. When I got there, she was just mean. She told me she was so much better than me because her parents are wealthy while mine aren't. She told me to look around at her house and realize that she was better than me in every single way. She was prettier, had more money, and was smarter. She didn't invite me to put our rivalry behind us. She was there to rub her family money in my face and try to make me feel terrible."

The more I heard about Ava, the less I liked her. However, just because she was an awful person didn't mean she needed to die. "Why did you stay?" I asked.

Her gaze slowly drifted over to Oliver. "Because he was there. And then, I fell asleep." She shrugged. "I woke up when the police arrived."

I stared at the young man while my dog continued to bark at the tree. "Gina!" she yelled. "Look! If I jump high enough I can almost get into the tree! When I do, I'm going to let this squirrel have it!"

"Oliver, it's been reported that you had words with a guy named Gabriel. Do you know him?"

He nodded, but wouldn't meet my gaze.

"Ava was cheating on you with him. Is that correct?"

"Yes."

"Okay, so riddle me this. If you're with Zoe, why do you care if she's with Gabriel?"

"I don't know." He groaned and placed his elbows on his knees, his head in his hands. "I just was so angry when I saw him."

Unfortunately, I wasn't buying that. "Do you want to know what I think?"

Zoe looked up at me and nodded, but Oliver wasn't interested in my hot take. I gave it anyway.

"I think that you, Oliver, wanted both your cake *and* pie. You didn't want to lose Ava or Zoe. You appreciate two beautiful women flocking to you, didn't you? Were you also seeing Terry?"

He didn't answer for a long moment, but then sat up and stared at me with his mouth in a thin, straight line. "Who is Terry?"

"The girl who attempted to drug Ava at the

party so she could have some time alone with you."

"No." He shook his head while Zoe gasped. "Absolutely not. I don't know her."

Interesting. Had Terry just been a slobbering idiot over a man who didn't even know she existed?

Zoe turned to Oliver, her brow furrowed as if she didn't fully understand him. "Is she right?" she asked. "Did you want both me and Ava? Because you told me you loved me." Daisy continued to bark and Zoe glanced over her shoulder. "Whose dog is that?"

"Mine," I muttered. "She's chasing squirrels."

Just then, the rodent jumped from the tree and ran across the lawn. It took Daisy a minute to realize what happened, but when she did, she pursued him to the next tree. Then it happened again. It did seem the squirrel was intentionally antagonizing her.

I turned my attention back to the kids. "You two are behaving horribly, but I need to ask you this: who do you think killed Ava?"

Both stared at each other a long moment, then shrugged. "I thought they had that guy, Jacob, in custody."

I shook my head and fisted my hands at my sides. Just someone insinuating he killed Ava made me see stars. "If he didn't do it, who did?"

"I don't know," Zoe said.

"Me neither," Oliver mumbled.

I didn't believe either of them.

Daisy came running over and sniffed their shoes while I fought the urge to punch them both in the face until one of them confessed.

Or was I just angry at my dog?

Yes, the two people in front of me were what I would consider young and dumb. But were they really killers?

Pointing at Oliver, I said, "The police are going to want to talk to you. It's probably in your best interest to not ignore them. And you, Zoe. I saw the boat in your yard. Have you spent a lot of time out on the water with your family?"

She nodded. "Yes. We love going out on the boat."

I smiled, filing the information away for later. "C'mon, Daisy." We headed back down the street toward the car.

"You seem mad, Gina," she said, trotting next to me.

"I am."

"Not at me though, right? Just at those two kissy-facers?"

"You told me that you would stay by my side, Daisy." I opened the door and pointed for her to get in. "And you didn't, so yes, I'm mad at you."

"But what about the squirrel?" she wailed as she jumped into the backseat. "You saw what he was doing! He was telling me I'm not a fast dog, that I couldn't catch him!"

I slammed the door and then slipped in behind the wheel. Oliver and Zoe stared at me from their bench. Making a fist, I banged it against the steering wheel, then laid my head back against the headrest.

"That looked like it hurt your hand," Daisy said. "Don't do it with the other one. I want to make sure you can still pet me when you aren't angry anymore."

I sighed as I stared at Oliver and Zoe. Did they think they'd outsmarted everyone? Or were they truly innocent? And if they were, who had killed Ava?

My phone buzzed in my pocket. After pulling it out, I glanced at the screen. Trevor.

I sent the call to voicemail, then tossed it on the seat.

"If that's my friend, Trevor, then you

should be nicer to him and tell him where you are," Daisy said. "Just an idea for the angry lady in the car."

She was right. I picked up the phone and texted him.

Meet me at my house in an hour.

CHAPTER 16

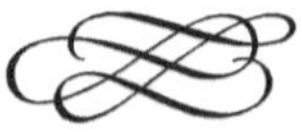

"WE HAVE to go get my dog!" Daisy yelled as we pulled into the driveway. "I need my Musty!"

I cursed under my breath, then said, "First, she's not yours. She's not a chew toy. Second, Trevor is going to be here at any moment. We don't have time to get her."

"Nooo! Mustard! My Mustard!"

Shutting my eyes for a long moment, I tried not to lose what little was left of my patience.

Daisy continued to wail. "Mustard! My friend! I'm coming for you!"

Just as I was about to back out my car, Trevor pulled in behind me.

"Trevor's here, Daisy. I can't leave."

"Dang it!"

"Besides, with Mustard gone, you'll get all of Trevor's attention. I thought you'd appreciate that."

Her tail swished back and forth. "I do! I do! Trevor! Trevor! Hi, Trevor!"

As he exited his truck, I studied him in the side mirror. The flexing and stretching of his hand was a good indicator he was quite angry, which didn't bode well for either of us. Usually, if one of us was having a bad day, the other was able to soothe over the emotions. But with both of us furious, we may ride into the afternoon and burn buildings.

"Hey," I said, opening the car door. "I can tell you're in a horrible mood, but just to warn you, so am I."

He stared at me a long moment, then shook his head and chuckled. "Okay, I get it. I'll try to keep my composure."

"Good. I don't think I'll be able to."

Trevor followed me into the house while Daisy jumped around his feet. "Hi, Trevor! Pet me! I'll make you feel better!"

"Where's the puppy?" he asked.

"You don't need that stupid puppy!" Daisy said. "You have me, Trevor! Whatever Gina tells you, I'm the best dog!"

"She's at Annabelle's," I replied. "I needed a babysitter, and Annabelle offered."

As we sat on the couch, Daisy took her place at Trevor's feet and stared up at him adoringly. "I love Trevor so much," she said. "He's my favorite. And I bet he'd understand the squirrel situation. He wouldn't be mad at me."

I rolled my eyes, not in the mood for her chatter.

"So, what's got you upset?" I asked, knowing full well Oliver not showing for his appointment fell somewhere in the conundrum of his bad mood.

"Well, Mallory is really on my butt about this case," he said. "Specifically, about you and Jacob. She's convinced you know exactly where he is and she wants him."

"She's wrong. I don't know."

"Can you reach him?"

I shook my head, hoping the lie didn't show on my face. The little phone—my lifeline to Jacob—burned in my pocket. I tended to lie pretty well most of the time.

Trevor cleared his throat. "I get the feeling you aren't being truthful, but I get it."

I remained stone-faced and said nothing. I'd go to jail myself before giving up Jacob.

"Moving on, Oliver didn't show up for the interview, so that's got my feathers ruffled."

"I can help you with that one," I said.

He furrowed his brow. "What do you mean?"

"I went to Flagstaff today to talk with Zoe and—"

"You went without me?"

"Yes, I did. I was feeling useless, so I decided to do something to clear my son's name."

He cursed under his breath, then returned his attention to me. "Okay, so what did Zoe have to say?"

"First, her family has a boat. She's spent a lot of time on it so she knows all about ropes. Second, I found her kissing Oliver."

"What?!"

"They were sucking face, Trevor," Daisy chimed in. "Sucking faces hard."

He leaned back against the cushions and stared up at the ceiling for a while. Despite my desire to spill everything I knew, I allowed him to simmer and take in the information and what it meant to the investigation.

"Well, I didn't see that coming," he muttered.

"Neither did I."

"The boat is interesting, but it doesn't mean she's guilty."

"I know, but she and Oliver making out... that's something that needs to be considered."

"Absolutely. What did they say when you caught them? And where did you find them?"

"They were in the park at the end of the street sitting on a bench," I replied. "In a nutshell, they've been together for a couple of months."

"Then why was Oliver ready to fight Gabriel for being at Ava's? Why did he care?"

"He didn't say," I replied. "My guess is he liked having two girlfriends who weren't particularly fond of each other. He liked the attention."

Trevor shook his head. "I don't get it."

I pulled out my phone and went to the school's website. "Look at him." I placed the screen in front of his face. "He's not some ladies' man. He's not some high-ranking athlete who's got a Rolodex of girls waiting to get into bed with him."

"Rolodex?" Trevor snorted.

Where in the world had that come from? I hadn't seen a Rolodex in two decades.

"Okay, so I've just dated myself, but you know what I mean," I huffed. "This is Oliver from Heywood with two pretty, smart, women who want to be with him. Why wouldn't he want to keep them around?"

"Going by that theory, he didn't kill Ava."

"I didn't say that. He could've started the night wanting both women. Maybe he saw the way Ava treated Zoe and he decided who was his top girl, and who he needed to eliminate."

Trevor gently stroked Daisy's head. "The way Ava treated Zoe? What does that mean?"

I repeated what Zoe had shared with me. "Ava wasn't a nice person."

"Okay, I can see Oliver being the killer, especially if Ava was as terrible to Zoe as you've described."

"Have you looked at Ava's social media?" I asked. "Her mom said she had an online stalker."

"It's on my list of things to do, but stop right there. When did you talk to Ava's mom?"

"I was at Sage Advice and she came in," I said. "We started chatting."

"Did you tell her who you were and what your son has been accused of?"

I shook my head. "I didn't *totally* lie. She suggested I was a true crime investigator, which isn't completely false, so I went with it."

"Oh, that's a lie," Daisy said. "Bad dogs lie,

Gina. I bet Trevor doesn't lie. He's such a good dog."

With a long sigh, I ignored her.

"Tell me about the social media deep dive that is on my list of things to do," Trevor said.

"Well, put a checkmark by it because it's done." I tapped on my phone, then brought up some of the posts. "Check it out. Obviously, someone didn't want to be identified. That's a throwaway handle."

He took my phone and scrolled through. "These are pretty awful. And why did she keep them up? Why not call the police?"

"Look at some of the responses from her friends, and then the way she answered them. I think she liked the attention."

After giving me a doubtful side-eye, he returned his focus to my phone. "Really? You think so?"

"She's been described as the center of everything more than once," I said. "She liked people noticing her. This falls within that line of thinking. Someone is horrible to her online. Her friends all come to her defense. The spotlight is on her."

"I wish I knew who this stalker was," he muttered. "I have some questions."

"Me, too." He handed me my phone and

we sat in silence for a long while. "Have you looked at her texts? I was told she received some awful pictures of male genitalia."

"I have looked through her phone, but I haven't seen anything like that. They've either been deleted or they never existed."

Interesting. Had Ava lied to her mother about the photos? Or had she received them and gotten rid of them? For some reason, the online harassment I'd witnessed on her account didn't feel male to me, although I couldn't explain why. Sending crotch shots and calling someone's butt big didn't seem to fit as one in the same person.

"What are you going to do about Oliver?" I asked.

"That's already in the works. He made me so angry today, I put out a BOLO for him and said his butt better be in a chair in the Sheriff's department before tomorrow morning."

"You put out a necktie on him?"

He rolled his eyes, my attempt at humor failing. "Be on the lookout, Gina."

"I know, I know. I wish you were in charge there," I replied. "You're honest and fair, unlike your boss."

"Running against her would be professional suicide. You know that. The second I announced my candidacy, she'd fire me."

"And maybe that wouldn't be a bad thing because you'd win against her."

"I don't know," he replied. "I like having a roof over my head and food in my fridge."

For a second, I almost suggested he move in with me if it came to him being homeless and hungry. The thought terrified me to the point my heart began racing. Trevor and I had a good thing going and I didn't want to do anything that may mess it up. Could we live together? We'd both been single for a long time. I was pretty set in my ways, and he seemed to be as well. Once when I was in grade school, I'd received a note I was supposed to take home to my father. It had read, *Gina doesn't play well with others*. I'd never given him the note, but the theme had continued to run through my life.

"I wouldn't mind my pretty Trevor moving in," Daisy said. "He's the best human. Trevor loves me *so* much."

Her upper lip moved, revealing some teeth. Was she trying to smile at him?

"Maybe I should convince Trevor to adopt me. He'd understand the things you don't, Gina. Like squirrels teasing me and the need for me to teach Mustard about bunny pee. Gosh, maybe he'd take both Mustard and me in! We could live without your tyrannical rules. I bet he doesn't care about pillows being torn apart."

I could only stare at her. A tyrant? Really? Maybe I'd been a little cranky the past few days, but that was because my son had been accused of murder. When Trevor left, Daisy and I would have a few words, and I really needed to collect Mustard from Annabelle. She'd most likely overstayed her welcome.

With a sigh, I picked up my phone again and went back to Ava's social media. The stalker's name still bothered me. 4Zr54Og9yt9E. A typical throwaway account for someone who didn't want to be recognized.

I gasped and shot to my feet. "Oh, my gosh," I whispered.

"What's wrong?" Trevor asked.

I slowly sank back to the cushion and sat next to him, shoulder to shoulder so he could share my screen. "Look at the stalkers' handle. What do you see there?"

He pursed his lips and shook his head. "I see random letters and numbers."

"Look at the capital letters," I urged.

After a few seconds, he inhaled sharply. "Zoe? Am I seeing that right?"

I nodded. "What do you think? Is she Ava's online stalker?"

We stared at each other for a long moment. "It makes sense," he replied. "Ava's rude and nasty and Zoe gets back at her online. It seems like it's someone anonymous, but Zoe's left a clever clue, as if to tease Ava."

"But what about the nude texts Ava claimed to have received? If we're right and this is Zoe hassling her online, who's sending the pictures?"

"Like I said, I didn't see anything like that on her phone. If they were real, there must be two different people stalking Ava," Trevor said. "We need to talk to Zoe and ask her about all of this." He continued to stroke Daisy's head as he furrowed his brow. "Ava invited Zoe to the party where she belittled her. If Zoe's the online stalker, could she have graduated to killer?"

"If she got pushed hard enough," I said. "She already tried taking Ava down a peg or two online. If Ava was as terrible to her as she told me... I'd say she just jumped to the level of number one suspect."

"And what do you think? Was she working

with Terry? Terry drugged the kids and Zoe finished her off?"

"I'm honestly not sure about Terry being involved in the murder at all," I said.

"That's quite the change of heart. Why? She admitted to buying the drugs at Hold Your Horses and using them at the party."

"First of all, Neither Zoe nor Oliver seemed to know her when I asked them about Terry today. Both looked confused."

"They could be playing dumb."

"Maybe, but it seemed genuine. I think Terry was honest when she said she'd tried to drug Ava so she could have time alone with Oliver. She knew nothing about Oliver and Zoe. Then when the kids started playing their water bottle game and she realized what was happening, she left."

"And the killer saw a perfect opening to get rid of Ava for good."

I nodded. "Yes, the night didn't start with Ava's death being planned."

"But was Zoe the killer?"

"Or maybe Oliver?"

"Probably both, Gina," Daisy said. "The face-suckers killed Ava."

CHAPTER 17

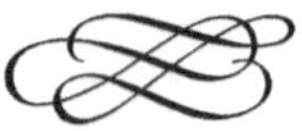

AFTER TREVOR LEFT at Mallory's calling, Daisy and I returned to Sage Advice to fetch Mustard. I really wanted to return to Flagstaff to speak to Zoe but that wouldn't be in the cards unless I dragged both dogs with me. Poor Mustard had been sick enough for one day.

"Jack! Mustard! Where are you?" Daisy yelled as she ran through the store. "Did you guys miss me? I had to help my human! Where are you?"

Annabelle smiled as I approached the counter. "Did you find the killer yet?"

"No." I sighed and sat down on one of her stools.

"Do you have a better idea of who it could be?"

"Also, no," I replied.

"Well, who do you think would want to, like, kill her?" Annabelle crossed her arms over her chest and eyed me curiously. "This isn't like you, Gina. Usually you're pretty focused."

I glanced around the store to make sure we were alone. "Between you and me, Ava wasn't a very likeable person. All of the suspects had motive. Everyone except Jacob, of course."

"So you need to find that one clue to nail them."

"And I have no idea what that clue is or how to locate it. Jacob doesn't remember anything, and for all I know, it's sitting right in front of my face." Frankly, I was a little tired of thinking about it, so I changed the subject. "How did Mustard do?"

"Oh, she's as sweet as they come," Annabelle said. Her face broke into a huge smile. "Just a doll."

"So she got along okay with Jack?"

"Yes. She seemed to bring out a little bit of puppy in the old man, which was nice to see. Even more so than Daisy does."

"That's great. I'm glad she wasn't a bother."

"Gina, are you going to keep her?" Annabelle asked.

I shook my head. "I plan to get her adopted. Why?"

Annabelle sighed. "I'm in love with that dog. I was thinking that maybe I could keep her?"

Well, I hadn't seen that one coming. I sat in stunned silence and stared at my friend.

"Jack also seems to like her, and Doug was playing with her earlier," Annabelle continued. "It seems like she'd be a great addition to our little family here."

"You know she's not going to be little forever, right?" I asked. "She's got some lab or Golden Retriever in her. I have no idea how big she's going to be."

"Oh, I know," she said. "Doug thought the same thing and said she'd, like, make a great jogging partner for him. Being outside and active helps him to stay sober, and Jack's just too old to keep up with him anymore. But Mustard... she'd be perfect."

It wasn't that I didn't trust Annabelle with the puppy. She was a good person with the most noble of intentions. However, Daisy had made it clear that the dog picked the human. The human didn't pick the dog. I wanted to make sure Mustard was placed somewhere she wanted to be.

Yet, I couldn't tell Annabelle I needed to check with Mustard and Daisy before committing.

"There's someone else who's interested in her," I blurted. "Let me call them and see if they still want her and I'll get back to you."

Her smile faded. "Okay, Gina. For some reason, I don't, like, totally believe you. Do you think I'm not capable of taking good care of her?"

"No! Of course not. I just... let me check with those other people, okay?"

She nodded then turned toward the back. "Jack! Mustard! Daisy! Come on!"

The herd of dogs came tearing down the back stairs. Poor Mustard was last and her little legs couldn't keep up. She rolled down the last few, then stood and yapped at everyone, as if her lack of coordination was our fault.

"Time to go home," I said as Daisy whizzed by me heading for the front door.

Mustard followed and I scooped her up. "Thanks again for watching her, Annabelle. I'll call you when I hear from the other people."

"What other people?" Daisy asked. I clipped on her leash then exited the store.

"I'll tell you when we get home," I whispered.

"Tell me now! What people? What's going on?"

"Later!" I hissed as we hurried toward the car. The last thing I needed was people staring at me while I had a conversation with my dog.

Once we were settled in the vehicle, I turned to Daisy. "Is Mustard feeling okay? Can you ask her to let you know if she's going to be sick? Then you can tell me and I'll pull over."

Daisy turned to the puppy, then back to me. "She says she's fine, and she'll let me know if she starts to feel yucky."

"Thanks." I started the car and we drove down Comfort Road, the main thoroughfare through Heywood. As we passed On The River, one of my favorite restaurants, I realized I hadn't been in recently to see Sally and have some of my favorite breakfast burritos. Maybe Trevor and I could go after we found out who killed Ava.

We arrived home without having to pull over to tend to Mustard's squeamish tummy. I scooped her from the car and followed Daisy to the front door. Once inside, I set down the puppy. She and Daisy ran for the kitchen while I plopped down on the couch.

Daisy trotted in a moment later. "Okay, Gina. What people do you have to talk to?

Does this have to do with finding Mustard a home?"

"Annabelle wants to adopt Mustard," I said. "I lied and told her someone else was interested in her so that I could have you speak to Mustard and see if she would be happy with Annabelle, Jack and Doug."

"Bad dogs lie, Gina."

"You've made me aware."

Mustard barked in the kitchen, then ran into the living room. As she yapped and jumped at Daisy's nose, my dog said, "I don't think that's a good idea."

"Well, it's not really up to us. It's up to Mustard. Can you please ask her?"

Daisy turned to the yapping puppy, who immediately settled down. As they had their silent conversation, I watched with fascination. Mustard's head swiveled back and forth as if she struggled to understand Daisy. My dog looked at her patiently. After a few moments, Daisy glanced at me. "She doesn't like Annabelle or Jack, so sorry! Nope. Mustard wants to stay here!"

Mustard trailed Daisy as they ran down the hallway. For some reason, I didn't believe Daisy, but I couldn't get Mustard's input myself.

What was I going to tell Annabelle? I couldn't say the other people were going to take her because she'd eventually find out I'd lied, and I couldn't give Mustard to her if she didn't want to be there. I'd have to come up with a plan, which basically came down to more lies.

As Daisy liked to say, I was a bad dog.

I leaned my head against the cushions and tried to figure out what my next steps should be and I was at a loss. Maybe I should go back to Bianca and talk to her again? I really didn't think of her as a suspect. I needed to write everything down.

I hurried into the kitchen to fetch my notepad and pen, then returned to the couch.

OLIVER – fell asleep at the party. Was dating both Ava and Zoe. Maybe killed Ava because of how awful she was to Zoe?

ZOE – possible online stalker and possible killer because Ava was so mean to her.

. . .

GABRIEL – in love with Ava. She broke up with him. Murdered her out of rage because of it. Also left the party and came back.

TERRY – could she have killed Ava to try to be with Oliver?

STALKER – if not Zoe, then who? And are they the possible killer?

SOMEWHERE, there had to be information that would lead me to the killer. Maybe DNA on the rope would be the telltale evidence. Except my son had been found holding the murder weapon. I swore under my breath, stood, and began pacing the living room.

Maybe I had to go back and consider Bianca as a viable suspect. She'd been there. If Ava had been as awful to her as she'd been to Zoe, maybe she'd killed her in a fit of rage.

Except, she'd been drugged as well. So that didn't fit. Unless she'd been faking it.

The idea stopped me in my tracks. How very clever to play the victim.

I needed more information on Bianca. It

seemed Jacob had spoken to her quite a bit at the party, so I pulled out my phone to call him.

My heart thundered and I gasped. I'd missed seven phone calls from him.

"Oh, my goodness," I whispered.

What had happened for him to call me seven times? Had Mallory found him?

Holding my breath, I called. He picked up on the second ring.

"Jacob? What's going on?" I asked. "Are you okay?"

"Mom! I remembered something from the night of the party!"

"What's that?" I asked. I sat down on the couch with a sigh of relief.

Daisy ran into the room. "Did I hear you say Jacob?"

I nodded.

"Jacob, it's Daisy! Come home, Jacob! I need my Jacob!"

"Well, I sort of remember the police arriving," Jacob replied. "But before that, I woke up for a second. It was kind of like I was in a dream. Someone was putting something in my hand and I opened my eyes. I saw yellow shoelaces."

CHAPTER 18

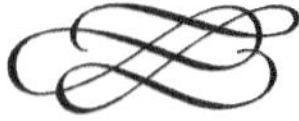

"Do you think that was the killer putting the rope in my hand?" he asked. "Because I do."

I shut my eyes. "Do you remember anything else about them?"

"Not really. I think they were on white shoes. I was pretty excited about the shoelaces, but I can tell in your voice that you aren't."

"No, I am!" I sat up and rubbed my forehead while attempting to drum up as much enthusiasm as him. "I'm glad bits and pieces are coming back to you. I'm just trying to figure out how this all fits together and how I can prove that you aren't the killer."

"Well, I don't know about that."

"Me neither."

"Find someone with yellow shoelaces."

We sat in silence for a moment as Daisy continued to whine for Jacob.

"Daisy misses you," I said.

"I miss her, too. You know, Mom, spring break is almost over and school starts soon. Am I going back?"

Of course I wanted him to return to college, but Mallory would meet him at his dorm room and arrest him. "Let's get you in the clear before we think about anything else. The second you come out of hiding, Mallory is going to pounce. We need to be careful."

"I hate this," he grumbled.

"So do I, honey, so do I." Then I recalled Brandy had been visiting. "How was Grandma?"

He snorted. "She was good, but don't ever call her that. She hates it. We played Uno."

"Did you win?"

"No, she did. I have a feeling she cheated, though. I can't prove it, but I was winning and then all of a sudden, I wasn't. It was fun though."

With her history, I had no doubt she'd deceived him.

"She said she'd come back tomorrow. Do you think you could come visit me?" he asked.

I'd have liked nothing more than to see him, but it was best for everyone if I remained clueless on where he was. "I can't, Jacob. Mallory may have me followed. If I don't know where you are, I can't lead her to you."

He sighed. "Okay. So, what are you going to do with the yellow shoelaces?"

"I'm not sure. I'll have to think about it."

We sat in silence for a long moment.

"Well, I guess I'll talk to you later." My son sounded defeated, and tears welled in my eyes. How was I going to find this killer?

"Sounds good, honey. Love you."

I hung up and stared into space while Daisy and Mustard wrestled in front of me.

As I considered the people I'd talked to in the investigation, I couldn't recall any of them having yellow shoelaces. However, I hadn't exactly been looking for them, either. Was it a unique thing to have, or was it a trend all the kids were following?

A knock sounded at the front door, which sent the dogs into a frenzy. When I opened it, I was surprised to find Trevor, who looked even angrier than before with his mouth set in a hard, fine line and his brow furrowed.

"Trevor doesn't look very happy," Daisy said. "In fact, he looks a bit scary. I don't think I like this Trevor."

"What's going on?" I asked.

"Mallory fired me."

My mouth hung open. "Really?"

"Yes. Can I come in?"

"Sorry. Of course." I stepped to the side as the dogs sniffed his feet. He walked into the living room and sat down on the floor, then was immediately attacked by Mustard and Daisy. When he laid down, they pounced.

"Trevor's face tastes good!" Daisy yelled. "We got him to smile, Gina! Trevor doesn't look scary anymore!"

"Alright, alright," he said, chuckling as he sat up. "You two need to back off."

"Dog kisses seemed to have improved your mood," I said.

"Maybe a little bit." He stood and sat next to me on the couch with a long sigh as he attempted to brush the dog hair from the front of his shirt. I knew from experience it was a futile effort.

"Why did you get canned?"

"She wanted me to arrest you for aiding and abetting a fugitive, and I told her I wouldn't. I didn't have any grounds to do that."

Uh oh. That didn't sound good. My freedom was the only thing that was going to save Jacob from her clutches. "I don't know where he is, Trevor."

"I know. I believe you."

"Should I be expecting another officer to come knocking at some point?"

He shook his head. "I don't think so. She demanded that a couple other guys head over here, and they all told her to go pound sand as well. Instead of de-escalating the situation, she fired me."

"To use you as an example of what could happen if they didn't do what she ordered?"

"Maybe. I guess so." He shrugged. "I don't think you have anything to worry about."

"What if she shows up here herself?"

He chuckled and shook his head. "Honestly, Gina, I think she's a little afraid of you. I don't think you have anything to worry about."

A little thrill traveled through me. Mallory was afraid of me? Great. I really enjoyed the thought. But that didn't mean she wouldn't try to throw me in jail, even if there was a hint of mutiny in the department. "I'm still a little worried."

He pulled out his phone and began typing. After hitting send, the device buzzed in his hand twice. A moment later, he shoved it back in his pocket. "There. I've asked the guys to let me know if she's going to accelerate her witch hunt."

"They'll call or something if she decides to come get me?"

"Yes. They said they would."

"Okay, that makes me feel a little bit better."

"Then let's get to work." He pulled out his phone again. "I had a bad feeling when I went back to the office, so I took pictures of the case file. I've got almost everything here on Ava's murder."

"Oh!" I sat up and took the phone. "Any autopsy reports yet? What about DNA on the rope? Anything?"

"The autopsy report came in." He reached over and swiped past a few documents. "That's it."

I quickly read over the report, which didn't yield anything I didn't already know, except the drug that was used. Ava had high amounts of Rohypnol in her blood, so I assumed Jacob had the same. I hadn't been officially notified by the emergency clinic yet. I retrieved my own phone and did a quick search on the drug. Loss of consciousness was one side effect, as well as amnesia. It came in a pill form that was both tasteless and odorless. Those kids had no chance of knowing they were drinking tainted water.

"The rope used was a waterski rope," Trevor said. "It was from the boat in the closed garage at the Willard house. We found lots of waterski equipment in the boat, as well as a rope that had been cut."

"Someone had been very intentional about how they were going to kill her," I mused. "Why not just hit her over the head with a rock? She wasn't going to fight back."

Trevor shrugged. "Maybe they didn't want things messy."

"Everyone had access to the boat. It was in a closed garage, so the killer had to know it was there, someone who was familiar with the Willards' property."

"That really doesn't narrow it down too much," Trevor said. "If we go by that reasoning, then Bianca, Oliver, and maybe Gabriel are all suspects. Zoe said it was her first time at the house, and it was the same for Jacob."

"You aren't seriously considering my son as

a suspect, are you?" I asked, completely offended. Who was this man I thought I knew so well?

"No. Just pointing out who was there and who hadn't been to the Willard's place before."

I nodded, feeling a bit better. "What about Terry? And Mrs. Willard had no idea Ava was also dating Gabriel. She wasn't surprised by it, but she didn't know he existed."

"That doesn't mean he'd never been to their house," Trevor said. "Mrs. Willard also didn't know about the party, and she may never have known if her daughter hadn't died there. Kids can be sneaky."

"But why would she bring Gabriel to her house here in Heywood when they both lived at the college in Flagstaff?"

"Off the top of my head, I was thinking she wanted time with Gabriel somewhere Oliver wouldn't find them. Or, perhaps she wanted to show off her house, like she did with Zoe. Or maybe, he was just wandering around and found the garage. We can't rule him out."

As I took all this in and let it churn, I watched Daisy and Mustard roll around on the carpet. Who had killed Ava? And how did I tell Trevor about the yellow shoelaces Jacob had seen? I'd just got done promising him I didn't know where my son was, which was true. But, I had lied by omission. The little burner phone in my pocket suddenly felt quite heavy.

Trevor wasn't with the Sheriff's Department any longer. Well, for now. I had a plan to get him reinstated, but this time, running the darn place.

I glanced over at him and admired his scruffy blond growth on his strong jaw. Did I see a few grays in there? Considering our age, it was a possibility.

Revealing my secret was a huge leap of faith. Did I trust Trevor? Very much so. However, this was my *son* we were discussing. I'd walk through cut glass barefoot while on fire for him. If I shared that I could contact Jacob and I had some evidence the police didn't and Trevor went to Mallory with it... not only would it break my heart, but I'd be beyond furious. Hell hath no fury like a mother protecting her child. Forget the women scorned. Their anger would be considered a walk in the park compared to the former.

Me sharing the news would be a huge jump in our relationship. It would show that I trusted him entirely, and frankly, that scared me. Having never been in a decent relationship, putting my faith—not to mention my son's future—fully in Trevor was frightening.

But we were now at the place in the investigation where I felt I had no choice.

"I have something to tell you." I set down both of our phones on the coffee table and turned to him.

"Oh, no," he groaned. "What now?"

"First, I don't know where Jacob is," I said. "I swear to you that's true."

"Okay," he replied. "I'm waiting for the other shoe to drop."

"I've been in contact with him," I said. "I actually spoke to him today."

"How?" Trevor asked. "Mallory has your phone tapped. His number hasn't come up at all."

I smiled and said, "Burner phones. Please don't ask anything else about it."

"Right." He rolled his eyes. "Should have figured that one out."

"Anyway, I spoke to him earlier, Trevor. He's remembered something about that night."

"What's that?"

"He recalled seeing someone wearing yellow shoelaces with white shoes when he was passed out, then he felt something in his hand.

He thinks it was the killer putting the rope in his palm."

Trevor shot to his feet and began pacing. "This is big news. Why didn't you tell me before?"

"Gina?" Daisy said. "There's something you should know." She trotted over and sat down.

"I didn't say anything because you're a cop and I didn't know if I could trust you," I replied.

Trevor arched a brow at me as his cheeks reddened. "Really, Gina? After all this time you didn't know if you could trust me?

"I just—"

"Gina!" Daisy shouted.

"I really can't believe this," Trevor muttered.

"Trevor, you have to put yourself in my position," I said. "I don't know who to trust. You're the police. Your department is looking for my son. Please try to understand."

"Gina!" Daisy yelled. "Gina, listen to me! It's important!"

"What?!" I shouted, losing my patience.

"The face suckers at the park!" Daisy replied. "One of them had yellow shoelaces!"

CHAPTER 19

I STARED at Daisy as Trevor asked, "What, what? Who are you yelling at?"

Having just told him about Jacob, I wasn't quite ready to share that I could talk to my dog.

"I'm... I'm sorry." Shaking my head, I hurried for the bedroom. "I'll be right back, Trevor. Don't leave."

Daisy trotted behind me, followed by Mustard, who kept yapping at Daisy and nipping at her feet.

When we entered the bedroom, I shut the door. "Who had the yellow shoelaces?" I hissed. "And why didn't you tell me about this before?"

"You never asked about yellow shoelaces,"

Daisy said as she jumped on the bed, then looked down at Mustard. "Stop biting me, you little monster. I'll put you back in the dumpster."

I sat down next to her on the bed and distinctly recalled her examining both Zoe and Oliver's shoes after the squirrel debacle. "Daisy, which one had the yellow shoelaces? Was it Zoe or Oliver?"

"Hmm... I don't remember. I wasn't looking at their faces. I was sniffing their shoes."

"Okay." I fisted my palms in my lap as I attempted to keep calm and not lose my patience. "There were two people sitting together on a bench. One was sitting on the left. The other was sitting on the right. Do you remember which person it was?"

"I don't really know my right from my left," Daisy replied. "And besides, if I'm looking at them from the back, isn't it different from looking at them from the front?"

I nodded, but I wanted to throttle Daisy. This was Jacob's life and it all hinged on a talking dog knowing her right from her left.

Mustard continued to bark at Daisy from the floor. I gently lifted her to my lap where she bit Daisy's nose.

"Ow, brat!" Daisy howled. "Someone should go drown you in a river!"

"Daisy!" I scolded. "That's a horrible thing to say!"

"I know." She laid down and placed her head on my lap. "I'm sorry, Mustard. That was mean. Just please quit biting me."

"Daisy, we have to figure out which person it was that was wearing yellow shoelaces. That's probably the killer. Jacob won't be in trouble anymore."

"That's a lot of pressure to put on me," she replied.

I ran my hand over her head. "I know it is, but you're the smartest dog around. We can get it figured out. Were there any smells that caught your attention when you were sniffing their shoes?"

"Maybe tacos?"

"Tacos?" I replied. "Really?"

"I don't know. Maybe I'm just thinking about how good tacos smell."

I sighed and shut my eyes for a moment. "Daisy, this is important. Please. Try to concentrate."

"Will you make tacos?"

"Yes. I'll make tacos."

As I stared at her, I wondered once again if

I was talking to myself. Was I having a conversation with my subconscious? Daisy and I had both been there, but perhaps dogs couldn't talk and I chatted away with myself but only thought it was the dog. This worried me.

And if that were the case, nothing made sense.

Although, tacos did sound delicious.

"Zoe was the girl with the curly hair, right?" Daisy asked.

"Yes." I noted that Mustard had fallen asleep in my lap. It always amazed me how puppies could go from one hundred miles per hour to zero in seconds, then right back again.

"Well, I don't think it was her," Daisy said. "The feet smelled like Jacob's. They were stinky. So I think it was the boy, Olive."

"His name's Oliver," I said, my insides buzzing with excitement.

"Well, Olive or Oliver, it still sounds like food and I'm hungry, Gina."

"Let's get you a snack in a minute," I replied. "So you think the yellow shoelaces were on the boy's feet, correct?"

"Yes, because they smelled like something died in them, just like Jacob's. And Jacob's a boy, so I think that maybe the boy's feet smelled the same as his."

Of course, none of this would ever stand up in court. A talking dog nailing the killer based on yellow shoelaces and stinky feet? Ridiculous.

However, I felt energized because it all fit.

Oliver killed Ava. Maybe she'd broken up with him that night and despite having Zoe, he decided if he couldn't have her, no one could.

Or maybe he murdered her in a fit of rage over Gabriel being present at the party.

He'd dated Ava for a long time, so he must have known about the boat. "There's only one way to find out," I muttered.

I marched back into the living room with Mustard in my arms. Grabbing my phone, I hurried back toward the bedroom. "I'm almost done!" I called to Trevor. "I'll be out in a minute!"

He cursed, but remained where he was. He'd been around long enough to accept my antics.

After sitting down on the bed, I called Ava's mother, Gwen. She picked up on the second ring.

"Gina?"

"Yes. How're you doing, Gwen?"

I immediately regretted the question. Her

child had died. She was in unrelenting pain, indescribable agony.

"I just took two muscle relaxers, so right now, I'm pretty numb," she slurred. "Did you find out who killed my baby?"

"Maybe," I replied. I had no way of proving any of it, though. "Can you tell me if Oliver ever went out on the boat with you and your family?"

"Many, many times," she said. "The kids even took it out by themselves every now and then. Why?"

"Just curious." Then another thought struck me. "Have you heard from Oliver at all? Has he been in touch?"

"No," she whispered, as if almost asleep. "I figured he was too distraught to talk to us."

Another nail in Oliver's coffin. If he hadn't been the killer, then I could only assume he'd want to speak with Ava's family. But I also imagined if he was the killer, seeing her parents would be very difficult, if not impossible. How would he look them in the face?

"I was going through Ava's things and found some love letters from him," Gwen continued. "He's a beautiful writer, Gina. It makes sense that he was majoring in English with an emphasis on writing and worked at the paper. It seemed as if he really enjoyed it."

"What did the letters to Ava say?"

"He loved her very much." She sighed. "They were very nice."

She sounded as if she were drifting off to sleep.

"Thanks for the information," I said. "Get some rest, Gwen. I'll keep you posted."

"Do you think it was him? Oliver? Do you think he killed my girl?"

I glanced at my dog who stared up at me with huge brown eyes. Based on what she'd shared with me I thought, yes, it was Oliver—but there wasn't any way to prove it. "I don't know," I replied. "But I'll be in touch soon."

After setting down the phone, I stared at Daisy again. "How am I going to show that Oliver murdered Ava?"

"I don't know," she said. "That's not my job."

"You could give me your input."

"Tacos. That's my input, Gina."

I needed evidence. But where would I find any? The police must have dusted the boat for prints. Had they found Oliver's? Even if they had though, it didn't matter. He'd been on the boat many times.

No, I needed something else... like shoes with yellow shoelaces. And a confession would be nice.

But how could I obtain all this evidence I so desperately wanted?

Suddenly, I wished Trevor had left. If so, I'd have time to think. Instead, I had to head back to the living room and attempt to explain my outburst without revealing my talking dog secret.

I stood with Mustard still in my arms.

"Gina?" Daisy said.

I turned to look at her before opening the bedroom door. "Yes?"

"I've been a bad dog," she said. "I lied."

"What did you lie about?" I hoped it wasn't the shoes.

"Mustard. She wants to go live with Annabelle. I lied to you and told you she didn't."

"Why would you do that?" I asked. Mustard barked at Daisy, then growled. I sat next to my dog again and stroked her head.

"Because I like her and want her for myself," Daisy said. "She's my little friend."

"Ah, I see," I said. "Well, I'm glad you told me the truth. What made you change your mind?"

"I felt bad for lying," she said. "And Mustard is angry at me because she likes Annabelle and her family. And then I remembered what you said about Mustard growing big. If she's mad at me and biting me now, what's she going to do when she's a lot bigger than me? Rip out my guts? So, I thought it was best to come clean."

"It always is," I muttered.

"You aren't angry?"

"Nope. I understand why you did what you did. Here's the thing, though, Daisy: we see Annabelle a lot. You'll be able to play with Mustard a few times a week."

"That makes me happy, Gina. I do like her."

The puppy crawled out of my arms and snuggled in next to Daisy. "I think she likes you, too."

"She's not mad at me anymore," Daisy said, licking the top of Mustard's head.

At least I had one of my problems solved. Mustard would go to Annabelle. I pulled out my phone and texted my friend before Daisy could change her mind.

In true Annabelle fashion, I received back a string of emojis that contained dogs, smiley faces and fireworks.

. . .

I TYPED:
I'll drop her over in the next couple of days.

NOW I just needed to figure out how to prove Oliver killed Ava. If I were a killer harboring evidence, where would I put it?

As a grown woman who spent way too much time thinking about murder and motives, I wouldn't keep anything anywhere near me. Heck, even my son was somewhere far away and I had no idea where.

But what if I were a lovestruck young adult?

My room, tucked away under a bed or hidden in some drawers.

I couldn't just march into Oliver's house and go through his room. The police could, but my contact in the department had just been fired.

An idea came to me—a terrible, terrible idea.

But one that may work.

I hurried to the living room and stood in front of Trevor, crossing my arms over my chest. "I need you to leave."

"You just yelled at me not to go anywhere!"

"I know, and I'm well aware I'm acting absolutely bonkers. But I'm about to do something highly illegal, Trevor. Since you're going to be the next sheriff of Heywood, I don't think you should be involved."

"The next sheriff of Heywood?" He shook his head.

"Yes. If you want to be. You'd make a great one."

"Gina, I feel like you've lost your mind."

"I kind of feel the same. I've drummed up a plan for you if you want to be sheriff, and a plan to catch the killer. You don't want to know about the latter, especially if you want to be the former."

CHAPTER 20

After Trevor left, I made a phone call. An hour later, my mother and father sat at my kitchen table sipping coffee. I absolutely hated having to involve them, but I couldn't pull off my plan. The only person I knew who could was Brandy, New York's Notorious Nanny.

I stared at the woman with the sharp blue eyes and long gray hair. Every fiber of my being detested I had to rely on her to clear Jacob's name, but I'd do anything to help him, and that included begging my mother for help.

"He's a nice kid," Brandy said. "You've done well, Gina."

"Thank you."

My father cleared his throat. "Why have

you summoned us? I know it's not to listen to us speak highly of Jacob."

I took a deep breath. "I need your help, Brandy."

She arched an eyebrow. "Oh, really? What do you want me to do?"

"I'd like you to break into a kids' house and dorm, look for certain items in his room, then take pictures of them and bring them back to me."

"You don't want me to steal anything?"

"No. It's evidence that will free Jacob. It needs to be left where it is so the police can find it."

"And how do you know it's there?" she asked.

"I don't. I'm hoping it is, though."

We sat quietly while she sipped her coffee and stared at the table. Finally, she said, "It's been a long time since I've done something like this. I'm not young anymore."

"Age is just a number," I shot back. "You're in shape. You won't have any problems."

"I feel great pressure from you."

"And I feel great pressure to find evidence to free Jacob." I stood and paced my small kitchen. "You know, Brandy, you were never there when I was a child. I didn't receive a birthday card, a Christmas present... nothing. I've never asked you for anything since I was two." I placed my hands on the table and glared at her. "You are the only person I know who can break into houses with ease and without detection. I am asking you to do this not for me, but for my son."

"I do like him," she said, smiling. "He's smart and has a great future ahead of him."

"Yes, he does. Spending the rest of his life in prison or on the run isn't going to do him any favors. So please, help him."

She nodded, then stared into her coffee cup again. "This isn't something I can do tonight. It's going to take planning."

"I understand."

"What are the addresses?"

In the hopes she'd say yes, I'd looked up Oliver's parents' address in Heywood, then also written down his dorm address at the college in Flagstaff. "The kids are on Spring Break. There won't be many people at the college." I hoped to convey that now would be the perfect time to sneak into the dorm undetected.

"Will the dorm be open?" she asked.

"Yes. There are some kids who don't go home or on trips."

Brandy glanced at my father, then smiled.

"Well, that's helpful. Change of plans. Why don't the three of us head to Flagstaff?"

~

DAISY HAD PROMISED me that she and Mustard would mind their manners before we left. Whether I believed her or not was a different story. I'd discover the truth when I returned.

My hands shook as I drove down the tree-lined highway to the college and my mother and father talked through their plan.

"You just have to pretend you're an old broad," my father, Theo, said. "It *will* work, Brandy. The idea is solid. Just be ancient and dumb. Society will take care of the rest."

Ancient and dumb weren't words I'd use to describe my elderly parents, but if that's what would free Jacob, then so be it. We pulled into the dorm parking lot and I shut off the car.

"Wait here, Gina," Dad said. "We'll take care of it."

After the car door slammed, I stared into space for a long moment. I couldn't let them 'take care of it.' For decades, I'd been holding the load of my life and responsibilities on my own. It felt unnatural and wrong to have someone else deal with my business.

Besides, what if they needed my help? Going into the lobby and waiting on the side-lines, ready to jump in, just in case, seemed like a smart move.

I hurried into the building and found them talking to a woman at the welcome desk. Brandy had her arm through my father's, her shoulders a little hunched. A few moments later, the student led them down the hall, leaving the desk unattended. Spring Break meant low employee and student count, which worked to our advantage.

My parents followed the woman slowly, my father even adding a little limp to his gait. Both were determined to appear as harmless as possible.

Rolling my eyes, I sat down and kept my gaze firmly on the hallway they'd gone down. *Please let this work.*

I waited for what seemed like hours. My leg bounced as I tried to appear nonchalant, as if a middle-aged woman sitting in a dorm lobby was a totally normal thing.

My phone buzzed in my pocket and I pulled it out. My mother.

The text read:

. . .

9-1-1! Down the right hallway at the end. Diversion. NOW!

I swore under my breath and followed the way they'd gone, where I immediately saw the problem. The student, my parents and a campus police officer were gathered outside one of the rooms. Dad and Brandy kept shaking their heads and pointing inside.

Before anyone could notice me, I turned down another hall and glanced around. She said they needed a diversion. What kind? Should I start a fire? Yell for help?

But then I saw exactly what was needed.

After running down to the end of the hallway, I pulled the fire alarm then walked quickly back the way I'd come. "Everyone out!" I yelled, banging on doors. "Let's go!"

I turned to where my parents stood. The campus police and the student hurried toward me. "Go clear the next floor!" I yelled. "Get everyone out!"

"Take care of them!" the cop ordered, hitching his thumb over his shoulder. "I don't think they belong in that room! They

said it's their grandson's but I'm not buying it!"

"I'll take care of it!" I shouted, running
past him.

My parents were already in the room.
While they rifled through the desk drawers, I
stayed in the doorway yelling at any remaining
person to vacate the building.

Glancing over my shoulder, I saw Brandy
snapping pictures of some papers on the desk
with her phone while Theo lifted the mattress
and quickly patted down the underside. He set
it down carefully, straightened the bedding,
and moved to the small wardrobe where he ran
his hands over a few garments of clothing.
Brandy tucked the papers back into one
drawer, then opened the other. She pulled out
a small book, flipped through a couple of
pages, then turned to me and smiled. "Bingo,"
she whispered.

As the fire alarm blared, I heard sirens in
the distance. "We better hurry," I said. "The
first responders are on the way."

"Theo, turn these pages for me," Brandy
said.

He hurried over and as soon as he'd flipped
a page, she snapped a picture. They both
grinned and moved together like a well-oiled

machine and I realized they were thoroughly enjoying the adrenaline and deception.

Brandy shoved the book back inside the drawer. As the three of us scanned the room for anything we'd forgotten and to make sure it didn't appear to have been tossed, I heard footsteps down the hall.

"We need to go!" I hissed. And just like that, my parents once again fell into their elderly roles of shuffling about.

Each of them linked arms with me, Brandy on my right, Theo on my left. Two firemen rushed past us just as we reached the lobby area, telling us to get out of the building.

"Moving as fast as I can, whippersnapper!" Theo yelled.

Both he and Brandy burst out into giggles as I led them out the door and straight to the car.

"That was a good one, Theo," Brandy said as they slid into the back seat. "Haven't heard the word whippersnapper in decades."

"What did you find?" I asked.

"I'm not sure," Brandy replied. "I saw Ava's name written in that diary, so I took a picture of every page that had writing on it."

It made sense to me that Oliver would keep a diary, especially if he was a poet and writer.

Considering his age, I imagined he'd put everything on a computer, but maybe all writers went old school every now and then. I hadn't seen a computer anywhere in the dorm room. Perhaps he had a laptop he took from school back to his parents' house?

As Brandy and Theo chatted about how good it felt to be "pulling jobs" again, I tried to ignore them and keep my mind focused on the next task: searching Oliver's room at his parents' home. After we reached Heywood proper, I took a small detour so we could see our next mark.

I slowed as we drove past it. "There it is," I said, tapping the window. The brown home with white trim stood off from the street. Tulips and daffodils lined the planters under the front window.

"Cute place," Brandy said. "I don't see any cameras. Do you, Theo?"

"Yup. Right there on the corner of the house. See it?"

"Oh, yes. So the house is wired up. Not good for me if I'm going to get in there undetected."

"Piece of cake, Brandy," my father said. "Just cut the wire going down the side of the house. Looks like they installed it themselves.

That's not attached to any sort of system that would alert authorities. A quick snip and no one will be the wiser."

"Hmm... do we know anything about their schedules?" Brandy asked.

I shook my head. "You'll have to do some homework on that."

After a quick U-turn at the end of the block, I drove by once more.

"No 'beware of dog' sign," Dad said.

"I'm not worried about dogs," Brandy replied. "They're easy. Right, Gina?"

I nodded, wishing I had Daisy with me. She could sniff around the property and locate the scent of any dogs the family may have. Just because there wasn't a sign didn't mean there weren't any.

"I'll come back tomorrow," Brandy said. "Let's go back to your house, Gina."

As I drove the short distance, I kept glancing in the rearview mirror. My father was staring out the window with a small smile on his face while my mother looked at her phone, likely at the pictures she'd taken.

"Find anything good?" I asked.

"Yes. A couple love poems about Ava, and also a diary entry of sorts where he talks about Ava cheating on him. He's not happy about it."

"Can you read it to me?" I asked.

"The poem or the entry?"

"Both."

"Well, I do have to say the poem isn't very good, but he gets an A for effort. It reads:

'Ava. The girl who stole my heart,
Has now broken it,
My pain is deep, so much so I can't breathe,
And I want to share it, to make her feel the same.'"

I KNEW LITTLE ABOUT POETRY, but my eyes widened at the last sentence. He wanted to make Ava feel the same breathless pain he had.

How? By wrapping a rope around her neck?

"What does the diary entry say?" I asked.

My mother cleared her throat. "'Ava is out with Gabriel tonight. She thinks I don't know, but I do. I want to follow them, to watch every move they make. I want to see every caress, the way her fingers wrap around his. Will her eyes light up when she looks at him? Does she love him more than she does me? And if that's the case, how do I live?'"

. . .

WE PULLED into the driveway and I sighed. Instead of being excited that we'd found evidence, I suddenly felt incredibly sad and drained.

There was no doubt in my mind Oliver had killed Ava. I had some proof, but not enough.

Gathering the rest of it would be up to Brandy.

CHAPTER 21

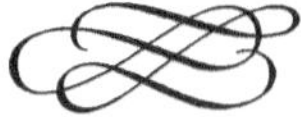

Two days passed while Brandy and Theo cased Oliver's house and I tried not to levitate out of my skin. Sitting by and waiting for things to happen wasn't my strong suit. If there was a problem, I took care of it. I didn't like relying on others, but in this case, I had no choice.

Trevor asked a lot of questions, which put even more strain on me, as well as our relationship. Knowing that his girlfriend and her family were currently involved in illegal activity wouldn't bode well for his future as the new Sheriff of Heywood. Well, that was my plan, anyway. He hadn't fully committed to the idea, but I sure had. Mallory had gone one step too far by implicating Jacob in Ava's murder. She was going down.

Daisy was on her best behavior, even when we dropped off Mustard at her new home. I promised the dogs we'd be by soon to play, but Daisy was still sad. She curled up on the bed and howled, "Musty! My pretty Musty! I miss you, my warm and cozy friend! I'll never forget our playtimes!"

If you asked me, it was a bit over the top. A drama queen to her core. She went on for hours. The hours turned into days, and I was about ready to find her a new home as well.

On the other hand, I was quite relieved Mustard had such a great family and I hoped she'd learn to like 80s music. Annabelle played nothing else.

In an effort to work off my nervous energy, my house became spotless.

Yet, nothing could've prepared me for the knock on my door Saturday night as I was vacuuming the living room for the second time. I opened it to find Brandy.

"Let's do this," she said, smiling.

"What does that mean?" I asked.

"It's time for you and me to head over to the Ledger home and look for the evidence that's going to nail Oliver."

I furrowed my brow. "I thought you and Dad were taking care of that."

"Theo's watching the Ledgers. Turns out they play poker at one of the casinos he likes." She pulled out her phone and pointed to it. "Your father will call me if they leave."

"And what about Oliver?" I asked.

"I just returned from the house. He's gone. Now, hustle it up before anyone goes back."

"I... I didn't think I would be involved in the breaking and entering," I stammered.

"Sorry, Gina." She sighed. "I can't go in on my own. Your dad's busy. Your brother is with your son. I need you and you need me, so let's call it some much needed mother / daughter time."

I snorted and shook my head. "I think the definition of mother / daughter time is shopping and pedicures, not burglary."

"It's only burglary if you take something. Now, grab your keys, lock up your house, and let's go."

I did as instructed, finding it weird that after all these years, Brandy was telling me what to do, as if I were a child.

Not going to lie, that grated on me. However, I had to save my own son, so I bit my lip and went along with her directions.

We pulled up in front of the darkened Ledger house. My heart thundered while I wiped my sweaty palms on my jeans. "I'm going to park on the next block," Brandy said. "We'll walk in."

After parking around the block, she turned to me. "We're out for a walk. Don't run, unless there's a dog or bear behind you."

"You aren't supposed to run from bears," I said.

"Then stay behind and get eaten, Gina." She threw her hands up. "Let's go. Act casual."

We exited the car and I stuffed my hands into my sweatshirt pocket, trailing after Brandy as we strolled down the street. I felt as if I were under a spotlight and sirens were blaring from my sneakers with each step I took.

When we arrived at the house, we walked up the camera-free side of the driveway and through the back gate. Before shutting it, I glanced over my shoulder. No nosey neighbors peeking through their curtains. Everything was dark and quiet.

I followed her around the back of the house where she handed me a pair of gloves and slipped on her own. "No fingerprints," she whispered, then fished out a pocket knife and quickly cut the camera wire she and Theo had discussed earlier.

"That should take care of the system," she said. "Even if they have cameras inside, which I doubt they do, it's been disabled."

We walked over to the sliding glass door while I stuffed my hands into the gloves. "Are you going to break it?" I whispered. "That will be loud!"

"Of course not." She pulled out a flathead screwdriver from her pocket and crouched down. After setting the flathead under the door, she pressed her palm up under the handle. In one swift motion, she pushed against the handle as well as on the screwdriver. The door popped upward and open with ease. I held my breath while waiting for sirens to blare. Nothing but quiet.

And a tabby cat who greeted us with a meow.

"If you ever live in a house with a sliding glass door, always put a stick in the tracks. If the Ledgers had one, we wouldn't have been able to get in." She stood to her full height and smiled. "Let's go."

I followed her inside, gently shut the door behind me and gave the cat a quick rub under the chin. I trailed her through the kitchen and living room. The streetlights gave us just enough glare for us to make our way without falling over furniture. Walking down the hallway, I felt like dozens of strangers were watching me from all the family photos lining the walls. In the dark, it was a little creepy.

Finding Oliver's room was easy. I was familiar with the smell of a room where a young man had been hanging out all day—a light scent of body odor mixed with cologne.

"I'll take the desk," Brandy said. "You look at the computer and inside the closet."

After grabbing the laptop, I sat down on the bed and opened it, but I didn't get far. A password was required and I had no idea of what to use. I gently shut the lid and set it aside.

Glancing around the room, I decided to check the closet.

Not too many clothes—mainly coats and sweaters. Since it was springtime, I assumed Oliver stored his winter clothing at his parents' house when not using it at the school. That's what Jacob did.

I opened a few boxes to find baby pictures and old clothing that looked to be much too small for him. His mom probably didn't have the heart to toss or donate them, as well as no room to hang anymore pictures.

A light illuminated the room and I turned to find Brandy with a flashlight in her mouth while she flipped through pages of paper. "I don't know what to do," I whispered.

She pulled the flashlight out from between her lips and shined it in my eyes. "Check the dresser drawers. Under the bed. If he's got evidence here, he's most likely hidden it."

Every little sound set fire to my nerves and I shook with worry that we'd be caught as I rifled through Oliver's dresser drawers. Not much to be found. A couple of condoms. Some dollar bills. Socks. T-shirts. Sweaters. As I felt around each drawer, I found nothing helpful. The cat watched us from the doorway. As our gazes met, he meowed, his tail swishing back and forth.

"Do you know a girl named Nina?" Brandy whispered.

I shook my head and turned around to find her standing by the window with a single piece of paper. "No. Why?"

Brandy shook her head. "Our boy, Oliver, seems to have tried to strangle her."

"What?!" I hissed. I stood behind her and looked over her shoulder.

.   .   .

Dear Oliver,

I don't know why I'm writing this to you instead of going to the police. I guess your threats worked. I won't go to the police, but I will if you ever hurt another girl again.

I was lucky to fight you off when you wrapped that belt around my neck. Really? That's how you treat a girl after she breaks up with you? You're such a loser, you'll always be alone. Always.

I hope you die in a fire. Watch your back, bud. I may make that happen.

Nina

"There's no date on it," Brandy whispered.

I snapped a quick picture, then said, "Put it back."

The golden boy, Oliver, seemed to have a horrible tarnish beneath his shiny surface. I sat on the bed, unable to believe that a woman had lived through someone trying to strangle her, but she hadn't gone to the police. Perhaps if she had, Ava would still be alive.

Relief washed through me. Once I turned the authorities onto the evidence they'd find in this home, Jacob would be free.

Brandy came and sat down next to me, placing her hand on my shoulder. "Unlike me, you're a good mom, Gina. We should get out of here."

Tears welled in my eyes as I turned to her. "Why didn't you ever let us know you were alive?"

She shrugged. "At first it was to protect you, but then I thought you'd be better off without me."

When my father had been the big drug kingpin in Northern Arizona, there'd been a turf war during which my mother's life had been threatened. She'd left to protect herself and her family. We'd never heard from her again.

I recalled all the nights I laid in bed, wishing for her presence. A simple hug, a squeeze of the hand, a kiss on the forehead. Something to let me know everything would be okay.

"You were wrong," I whispered. "We needed you."

"I understand that now," she said. "I wish I had then."

With a nod, I stood. I hated messy relationships and tended to avoid them. The conversation with Brandy wasn't any different.

"Let's go," Brandy urged. She rose from the bed and headed out of the bedroom. I took once last glance around.

The bed.

I hadn't checked under the bed.

After dropping to my knees, I lifted the comforter.

And there, I found a pair of white shoes with yellow shoelaces. As I snapped a picture of them the smell made my eyes water. Daisy hadn't been lying when she said the odor resembled something dead. With a smile, I stood and followed my mother.

She came to a halt in the hallway, then quickly turned back toward me. After she pushed me into Oliver's bedroom, we hid behind the door. Just then, I heard footsteps coming and I shut my eyes, hoping we'd make it out of the house without being shot or having the police called.

I glanced over at Brandy. She stood with the baseball bat raised above her shoulders. Where in the world had she picked it up? I hadn't noticed one anywhere in the bedroom, but she had.

The lights went on, and a second later, Brandy jumped from behind the door and smashed the baseball bat over someone's head.

"Let's go," she ordered, dropping the bat. I came out from behind the door to see Oliver lying face down on the carpet. I couldn't seem to move. I'd wanted him to go to prison if he'd killed Ava, which by all the evidence we'd found, he had. I hadn't wanted his brains knocked around.

Brandy disappeared down the hallway while I leaned over to check for a pulse. He groaned as my fingers found the steady beat in his throat. With a sigh of relief, I stood and hurried from the room to find my mother.

I discovered her in the master bedroom taking some jewelry and cash.

"What are you doing?" I hissed. "We agreed you wouldn't take anything!"

"We have to make it look like he walked in on a burglary," she replied calmly.

"Why can't we just leave?" I glanced over my shoulder, praying Oliver didn't wake.

She sighed and shook her head. "Gina, if we don't take things, then Oliver will be able to say the evidence was planted when the police find it. We need to make it look like the two aren't related. Now, please, go grab that laptop on the dresser over there. Leave Oliver's though, just in case there's damning evidence on it."

I did as instructed, my mind whirling with attempts to reconcile that what we were doing was for the greater goal: making sure Oliver went to prison for murder.

Moments later, Brandy motioned me to follow her out of the house. As we hurried down the street, I decided to wait a day or two to tell Trevor about the evidence in the Ledger home. The break-in couldn't correspond with its discovery, and I imagined Oliver wouldn't think about moving or destroying any of it. Brandy may have hit him hard enough to warrant a hospital stay. I took some deep breaths as we drove home. My hands wouldn't stop shaking and my stomach felt as if I'd eaten rocks for dinner.

But we had our killer, and now I was ready to move on to my next project of getting Trevor elected as sheriff.

Mallory was done.

EPILOGUE

TWO MONTHS HAD PASSED since we'd solved Ava's murder. Brandy and I were on terms. I wouldn't say they were good or bad. She didn't barge into my life and I left her alone. We connected every now and then. My brother, Vic, was much closer to her, and I was fine with that. He'd carried a lot of guilt for decades, thinking he was the reason she'd left.

I'd learned Brandy had fenced the stolen items from the Ledger house. I never asked how much she'd ended up with, but I did discover she and my father were taking a month-long cruise. I tried to convince myself that it was payment for them getting Jacob off, but it all felt very dirty to me. I finally came to the conclusion that my family preferred to operate on the wrong side of the law and there was little I could do about it, except keep my son and me on the right side.

Jacob had returned to college, Oliver hadn't. A search warrant had been executed and all the evidence discovered. He hadn't put up much of a fight and had eventually confessed. Mallory got on the local news, praising her department's prowess and her own ability to lead them to victory.

My goals hadn't changed: I was going to get Mallory out of office. Trevor had finally agreed to throw his hat in for the position, but only after I told him that I'd find a drunk monkey to run against her if he didn't. He still worried about being good enough for the job, regardless of my faith in him. Maybe I didn't know exactly what it took to be the sheriff of Heywood, but his integrity and honesty had to count for something. His desire to do what was right was more ethical than Mallory's need to do what was easiest.

Daisy and I stood outside the restaurant, On The River, handing out flyers to introduce people to Trevor. A lot of our population knew him or was at least familiar with him, but I wanted everyone to understand what a good guy he was. Sally, the owner and my friend, was also placing flyers on every table. I handed them out at my business, File It Away, and Annabelle did her part from Sage Advice. Adrienne over at Never Quit Wining also said she'd allow some to be available at her store. My goal was to have every place of business handing out flyers supporting Trevor.

"Gina, it's really hot," Daisy complained. "And I'm tired of looking cute. I want a nap."

"Please keep it up for just a while longer," I said. "Do that thing where you perk your ears and tilt your head. People seem to love that."

It was the perfect trap. They saw Daisy, smiled, asked if they could pet her, then as they did, I talked about Trevor for Sheriff. I still needed a catchy phrase, but I'd work on that. "Here comes another group," I whispered. "Wag your tail, too."

Daisy did as I asked, and the four people came over to greet her. As they oohed and ahhed over her, I talked about having a sheriff with integrity. "I've put together a list of his accomplishments," I said, handing each one a paper. "Many of the murders here in town were solved by him, and him alone."

"With our help," Daisy chimed in. "She's the super sleuth and I have the super sniffer!"

"That's impressive," one of the men said. "Thanks for letting us know."

"If you're looking for honesty and integrity in such an important position, please make sure to vote for Trevor," I said, smiling.

All this socializing was wearing me down. And Daisy was right—the summer sun beat down on us relentlessly. In fact, I could also use a nap.

The group went into On The River and I turned to Daisy. "Let's pack it up. I'm really tired."

"It's about time," she groaned. "I'm so over this being cute stuff. Don't make me do this again tomorrow."

"We want Trevor as our sheriff, don't we?"

Daisy stilled, her gaze on the parking lot. "Uh oh," she whispered. "Here comes trouble."

I glanced up to see Sheriff Mallory walking toward me. Short and stalky with black hair, she smiled—the kind of smile an alligator would give someone before eating them.

"Gina Dunner," she said. "Do you have a permit to be handing out these flyers?"

"Do I need a permit to stand on private property with the owner's permission?" I retorted. "I don't think so."

She grabbed the paper from my hand and looked at it. "Ah, Trevor for Sheriff. That's a lost cause."

I ripped it from her hand. "No, it's not. He's much better suited for the job than you are."

As she grinned again, she leaned in close. "If you think for a second that I'm going to allow you to take this job from me, you couldn't be more wrong. If you don't back off now, I'll make sure you never see the light of day, Ms. Dunner."

"Is that a threat?" I asked, narrowing my gaze.

She threw her head back and laughed. "Of course not. I'm an upstanding officer of the law, Ms. Dunner. How dare you even think such a thing?"

"You're a psychopath," I retorted. "And I'm going to get Trevor voted in if it's the last thing I do."

"I've given you my input on this matter," she said. "Have a great day."

While she walked back toward her car, Daisy made a snorting sound. "What does that mean?"

"Which part?"

"Where you'll never see the light of day?

Does that mean she's going to kill you and bury your body in the deep, dark woods?"

"I'm not sure what she meant by that," I said. "Let's go home."

Despite the heat, a chill ran down my spine. Mallory was coming for me. I'd have to watch my back because I'd put nothing past her.

But one thing was certain: I wouldn't allow her to deter me. I'd get her out of office no matter what she tried to do to me.

investigations. Danger and hilarity ensues as the crazy duo follow the clues to discover the killers.

The Tri-Town Murders

(Small town contemporary cozies)

Follow newspaper reporter Tilly and her group of fun, quirky friends as they solve murders in a fictional, small town in California.

ABOUT THE AUTHOR

USA Today bestselling author Carly Winter writes fun, small town cozy mysteries, always with a dash of humor and quirky characters. When not writing, you can find her spending time with her family, on a Pilates reformer or enjoying the fantastic Arizona weather (except summer - she doesn't like summer). She does like dogs, wine and chocolate and wishes Christmas happened twice a year.

To be notified of new releases, book recommendations, to learn more about Carly and for your chance to win giveaways, please visit: CarlyWinterCozyMysteries.com